To Be Loved

To Be Loved

Barbara Yoder

Printed in the United States of America

Publishing services by Selah Publishing Group, LLC, Tennessee. The views expressed or implied in this work do not necessarily reflect those of Selah Publishing.

ISBN 978-1-58930-286-0

Library of Congress Control Number: 2012917585

Acknowledgements

Thank you to my husband, for encouraging me for supporting me and loving me.

Thanks to my editor Mary Schwartz Henke for all her encouragement and hard work.

Thanks to my amazing daughter Melissa for doing the design work.

Thanks to Emily Rose for doing a great job on the photography.

I must also mention my three sons Justin, Jonathan, & Jaden who bring me much joy.

I never dreamed the writing of this book would be so long. I am thankful it is finally here. I have learned so much during my journey to this moment and am so grateful to God for the many things He taught me. May I apply it to my life to be a blessing to all those around me.

Chapter One

Rose planted her bare feet firmly on the wagon floor; she gripped the reins of the Belgian horses she was driving. She loved a challenge; a test of her physical strength, but this was proving to be too much. "Slow down boys," she called, hoping the load of loose hay she was hauling would stay intact. Instinctively, knowing they were headed for home, the horses continued to pick up the pace. The steel wheels of the hay wagon bounced roughly over the ruts in the lane. Rose dug her heels in hard against the rough sawn planks of the wagon floor her callused feet protecting her from harsh slivers.

"Whoa, Charlie! Whoa, Max," she commanded with urgency, knowing they were fast approaching a sharp turn in the lane ahead. Panicking, both at the thought of what her father would do to her and at the thought of losing an entire load of hay, the better part of a day's work, she pulled desperately on the reins exerting every ounce of her strength; "I have got to slow them down or I will never make the turn!" She pulled hard on the right rein trying to keep the horses from taking the turn too sharply to the left, and even then only narrowly missing the corner fence post.

"Whoa, Charlie!" she yelled; as she felt the load of hay behind her begin to slide off the wagon. "Oh no! Look at what you did!" she scolded as she succeeded in slowing the team to a brisk trot. Charlie's nostrils flared and his sides heaved as Rose continued scolding. "You are naughty! You just got me in a lot of trouble!"

Rose looked back with a sinking heart at the pile of hay left lying beside the lane. Dreading the response of her father and knowing she couldn't delay the inevitable, she headed toward the barn.

"What happened?" Father demanded harshly taking in the wagon only half full of hay.

Rose shrunk back fearfully at his angry tone. She knew the flogging the horses would receive if she told the truth. "I was going too fast," she lied, bracing herself for the reprimanding she knew was coming.

"Any *gute* Amish *matel* would have enough sense not to run horses with a load of hay!" Dad remarked, with irritation.

Rose stared down at her torn skirt and bare feet swallowing back the tears as Dad continued to lecture her. It was just an accident. He does not even care whether or not I am ok, she thought bitterly.

"Grab a fork and pitch the hay over the fence so the cows can feed on it before you come in for supper," Dad ordered before turning and walking away.

Rose gripped the smooth handle of the old barn fork and pitched a mound of fresh cut hay over the fence. Forkful after forkful it flew over the fence until Rose's palms felt sore and her shoulders ached. She knew quitting was not an option. Her father Eli Miller, was a hard man. He took great pride in the old farm that had been in his family for generations. He knew every rock and stump like the back of his hand. Everything on his farm was under his control down to the weeds that were plucked out of the fence lines every spring. Eli Miller also expected unquestioned submission from his family, including his wife of forty-five years.

"Whew! Am I ever glad that is done!" said Rose as she threw the last forkful of hay over the fence. Putting the fork back in the barn, she grabbed Abby's bridle and saddle. "Let's go for a ride, Abby," she said as she fastened the bridle strap on her favorite riding horse. Regardless of the consequences, she wanted to get away for a bit.

The evening sun shone down warmly on Rose's back as she leaned forward in the saddle, urging her horse to go faster. She loved the feel of the wind in her face and the sound of the pounding hooves beneath her. After a dusty day in the hayfields, the wind, even though humid, felt refreshing. Spotting the creek up ahead, Rose knew she should begin to slow down, but maybe just for tonight she and Abby could jump the creek and keep going. Knowing that wasn't possible, Rose pulled gently on the reins. "Whoa, Abby," she spoke softly to her horse, "Would you like a drink girl?" Slipping from the saddle she took the reins and led Abby to the edge of the water. Plopping down beside the creek, she dangled her feet in the cool refreshing water as she waited for Abby to drink her fill. Rose sighed with contentment as she stretched out on the soft green grass. This was her favorite spot. She loved the calm, quiet solitude, the soothing sound of the water trickling over the rocks, and the old oak trees that lined the creek and formed a shadowy, green canopy above her. Back here, she could get away from the business of the farm. Rose sighed tiredly; it was an extra hard summer. Her two older brothers had gotten married this past spring and moved to their own farms leaving all the farm work to Rose and her younger sister, Katie. They were the last two of the Miller clan. There had been a dozen of them in all, seven girls and five boys. One by one they had gotten married and moved to farms of their own in the surrounding community.

"We had better get back," Rose said, looking at Abby and patting her soft black nose. Sometimes she felt like Abby was the only one who really understood her. Rose wished she could talk to mom about dad's bad moods. "Why did he have to be so harsh anyhow?" She muttered bitterly reaching up and pulling herself into the saddle, reluctant to head back to the farm. Rose looked at the sun, now low in the evening sky, casting long shadows across the fields; thankful the long hard day was finally ending.

"Oh, no!" she groaned as she reached the gate heading back into the barnyard. It stood wide open. "How could I have forgotten to close the gate?" she scolded herself. The cows were heading quickly into the newly mowed hay field.

Digging her heels in hard, Rose chased after the wayward cattle, hoping she could have them back in their right pasture field before Dad saw what had happened. But after several failed attempts at rounding them up, Rose was forced to call the trusty farm dog, Seven, to assist her, in getting the unruly cattle back to pasture.

Exhausted, Rose put Abby in her corral and headed for the house knowing she would be in trouble with Dad for the second time that day, her heart sank. She slipped quietly into the small washroom just off the kitchen, noting the house was silent except for the sound of spoons clinking against the dinner plates. Pumping fresh water into the washbasin, Rose slowly washed her face and hands, wishing desperately that she would not have to face her father. Drying her hands and face she hung up the towel, and stepped into the kitchen.

"Rose!" said Dad his voice harsh. Shoving his chair back from the table he came to stand in front of her, his six foot frame towering over her making Rose quiver with fear.

"Yah," answered Rose keeping her eyes lowered as a sign of submission.

"Where were you?" he demanded.

"I rode Abby back to the creek."

"Why did you leave the gate open?" he demanded.

"I forgot," replied Rose quietly.

"Then you can forget supper. Maybe that will help repay for the damage the cows done to the hay. Now go to your room!" Turning, he walked back to the table to finish his supper.

Rose stumbled and quickly fled up the stairs to her bedroom. It had been a long hot afternoon of working in the fields and putting up hay. She had been looking forward to one of Mom's delicious suppers of hot stew and fresh biscuits, but right now Rose did not think she could eat a bite if she tried.

Closing the door behind her, she flung herself across the bed and stared out the window. This time there were no tears, only anger at her father for never giving her any words of appreciation for the all the hard work she did around the farm. "This is the thanks I get!" she muttered punching her pillow. Rose lay there a long time, regretting not staying down by the creek or better yet wishing she would have kept going and not looked back, but where would she go? The few dollars she had to her name would not get her very far. Every penny she earned had to be given to her father and that is the way it would be until she turned twenty-one.

Getting up from the bed, Rose walked over to the window. The sun had set and the first stars of the evening were twinkling in the sky. Just then a soft knock sounded at the door. Rose smiled knowing it would be her younger sister, Katie. "Come in," she called softly.

Katie opened the door and held up a cookie and a glass of milk. "I thought you might be hungry."

Rose shrugged. "I was so angry at Dad, I did not think about it too much."

"Oh Rose, why did you ride away like that without asking?"

"Oh, come on!" snapped Rose. "I only rode to the back of the farm; I did not commit a crime."

"I know, but you have to be careful when Dad is in a bad mood," admonished Katie.

"I am twenty years old," snapped Rose. "I should not have to ask permission to go anywhere! I am so sick of being told what I can and cannot do! I wish I could trade lives with Kristen," referring to their non-Amish neighbor with whom she was secretly best friends. "Just think," continued Rose, "in a couple weeks Kristen is leaving to go to college. She will get to be on her own and do what she wants."

"Are you and Kristen still meeting secretly?" asked Katie disapprovingly.

"When we have a chance," Rose admitted defiantly.

"One of these times you are going to get caught," warned Katie.

Rose shrugged carelessly. "I do not care."

Katie sighed knowing it was useless to argue with Rose. "I did hear Dad tell Mom that he is ready to rent out the farm next summer," said Katie hoping the news would put Rose in a better mood.

"It is about time," grunted Rose.

"Well, I better go to bed before Dad hears us talking," said Katie. "Oh, yes, I did bring you a big pitcher of warm water. I thought you might like to wash up after all the dust in the hay fields today."

"Thank you," said Rose gratefully.

Lighting the small oil lamp, Rose poured the water into the porcelain washbasin.

"I guess a bird bath is better than nothing," she sighed as she scrubbed her body with the now cool water and a sponge. Finished with her bath, Rose slipped into a homemade cotton nightgown and stepped in front of the small mirror to comb her hair. Removing her white head covering she took the hairpins out of the bun on top her head; and placed her covering carefully on her dresser, the covering was the most important part of her attire. It was worn as a prayer covering and for a wife it was worn as a sign of submission to her husband. It was even worn to bed. She was never to be found without it, unless she was combing or washing her hair. Rose loved her long hair that spilled down past her waist. Not that it mattered if she didn't; she was not allowed to cut her hair.

Leaning forward, Rose studied her reflection in the mirror. Her light brown hair looked golden in the lamplight and her eyes a deep blue against her deeply tanned skin. "Not too bad," she muttered. But, was she, someone who would be considered pretty? She wondered. Mom always said that inner beauty was what counted the most; Rose remembered her mother's admonishing as she crawled into bed. However it would be nice to be told one was beautiful, Rose thought longingly.

Rose looked around the tiny room. It was a typical Amish girl's bedroom. Plain white walls, hardwood floors, little white curtains over the two small windows, an old dresser with a porcelain pitcher and bowl, a small mirror hanging above it, and a braided rug beside the bed. The old-fashioned four-poster bed was adorned with one of Mother's beautiful handmade quilts and a little nightstand beside her bed with a lamp and a bible completed the look.

The Bible. Rose reached over and picked it up. She felt guilty, realizing it had been several weeks since she had read from it. Letting it fall open, Rose began reading.

The Lord is my Shepherd, I shall not want, He makes me to lie down in green pastures, He leads me beside still waters, He restores my soul. The familiar words of the twenty-third Psalm were soothing, compelling Rose read to on. Several minutes later she finished the chapter and closed the book laying it back on her nightstand.

"What does it mean spiritually?" she wondered remembering the phrase: *He leads me beside the still waters.* "Is God leading me?" she asked herself. Probably not, she decided as she thought about her anger toward her father. God could not be with someone who was angry and rebellious. God loved people like Katie, who were always good and obedient. I wish I could be good enough for God, she thought to herself, feeling heavy-hearted. Rose wished she knew if she were going to '*dwell in the presence of the Lord forever*' like the Psalmist David. The thought of eternity sent a chill up her spine. Where would she spend it? Tired and not wanting to think about it, Rose leaned over and blew out the small orange flame in the oil lamp leaving the room in darkness.

Chapter Two

"We got the third cutting of hay into the barn without it getting rained on," said Dad looking across the supper table at Mom.

"That is *gute*," replied Mom smiling. "Now maybe you can get some *ruhe*."

"Yah you're right," he agreed. "Next year I'll rent the fields out."

Rose sighed with relief as she listened to her parent's conversation. It would be several months before the corn was ready to husk. She was ready for a break from working in the fields.

"What's the dog barking about?" asked Dad interrupting her thoughts.

Rose got up from the table and looked out the window. "The Nelson's are here," she answered referring to their non-Amish next-door neighbors.

"Go out and see what they want!" ordered Dad impatiently.

Rose hurried outside. She knew Dad didn't like "outsiders" as he referred to them, in their home.

"Hi Rose," greeted Mrs. Nelson. "How are you?"

"I am fine," replied Rose shyly.

"I'm afraid I have bad news for you," said Mrs. Nelson. "We just received a message for you from your relatives in Pennsylvania that a Norman Miller and his wife were killed in a car accident this afternoon. Here is a number for you to call for more information," she said handing Rose a piece of notepaper.

Rose gasped with the surprise. "Why, they were here just two weeks ago!" she exclaimed. "He is Dad's first cousin."

"I'm sorry to bring you such bad news," said Mrs. Nelson sympathetically. "Oh yes, I almost forgot, Kristen wanted to know if you could meet her tonight?"

Rose glanced nervously over her shoulder hoping no one had heard. "Tell her I will try, and thank you so much for bringing the message over." Turning quickly and hurrying back into the house Rose relayed the message to her parents.

"Norman was my age," Dad reminisced. "We grew up together. We used to spend the night at Grandpa's house and then he would take us fishing. And now he is gone," mused Dad stroking his long gray beard.

"I feel so *schlim* for the little children," said Mom, sadly wiping her tears.

"Oh, poor Sarah! What will she do?" Katie fretted worrying about her favorite cousin.

"Finish eating, Rose, so you can go over to the Nelson's to make some phone calls. Find out when the funeral is, and don't be long talking to them Nelson kids either!" commanded Dad.

Rose agreed obediently hurrying to finish her supper.

"May I please go to the funeral, too?" Katie begged. "Sarah is my best friend."

"Who would do the chores?" asked Dad.

"I can do them," volunteered Rose.

Dad hesitated a moment. "I suppose you could," he agreed. "If you need anything you can get Joseph to help you," referring to Rose's older brother who lived across the field.

"Are you sure you do not want to go too?" asked Mom.

"I will be fine here," said Rose confidently, feeling excited at the prospect of having a couple of days to herself. Funerals made her think of eternity, giving her a sick feeling in the pit of her stomach.

"You go on ahead and make the phone calls," Mom instructed after supper. "Katie and I will wash dishes."

Rose could hardly believe her good fortune! Dad had picked her to go to the Nelsons. She could hardly wait to see Kristen. She and Kristen had been best friends since first grade. Kristen had come with her Mother to the Miller's farm to buy eggs, milk, and produce. Rose thought about how she would take Kristen to the barn to show her the newborn kittens, and to help gather eggs. Sometimes Kristen's older brother, Lane, would accompany them and the three of them would play in the hayloft. Rose smiled as she thought about Lane and the crush she had, had on him, and perhaps still did, even though she had not seen him since he left to join the military. She thought he was the cutest boy she had ever seen, with his black wavy hair and dark brown eyes. Lane had been dangerous and exciting, so different from the plain boys in her own community. But when she had finished school, Dad had insisted that the friendship between her and the Nelson kids stop, remembered Rose. "You need to get to work," were his exact words. "Being friends with outsiders is not a good idea," he'd continued. "The only contact with outsiders should be for business reasons," he finished. Despite Dad's rules Rose and Kristen kept their friendship. They began meeting by the old oak tree back by the creek sometimes hiding letters for each other in a special crack in the old tree that they laughingly referred to as their tree mail.

"Please tell me you are coming to my house!" called Kristen pulling her car alongside Rose.

"Yes, I am," smiled Rose. "I have to make a few phone calls."

"Hop in then," invited Kristen.

"It must be so much fun to drive a car." said Rose sliding into the passenger seat.

"Oh yes, it is," said Kristen enthusiastically. "Maybe someday I could teach you."

"I could get away with that," giggled Rose. "Besides, I would be too scared to try."

"Oh, Rose, you're so silly!" laughed Kristen. You're in more danger riding Abby!" Parking the car in the garage, Kristen got out. "Make your phone calls, but hurry, so you can come up to my room and we can talk," she said as she led the way into the kitchen.

Rose looked around the brightly colored kitchen. Everything here was much different than her simple home. The pale yellow walls were lined with a bold border of big, bright sunflowers, contrasting the plain white walls and dark cupboards so familiar in her own home. Rose loved all the bright colors, but she knew that her parents believed that living a plain and simple life was equivalent to godliness.

Rose could only remember of a few times that she had used a phone. She called the numbers on the list carefully following her father's instructions, sighing with relief when the last number was called. Putting the paper in her pocket, she hurried upstairs to join Kristen.

"I can hardly believe I'll be moving out in two weeks," said Kristen showing Rose the stacks of packed boxes. "I know I'm going to get homesick. I'll miss you so much," she continued. "Everything will be changed when I get back. You'll probably be married and having babies. I feel sad that we're growing up."

Rose nodded, feeling emotions she didn't like. "You probably will not come back."

Kristen sighed. "Yes, you're probably right, but we'll always be best friends, right?"

Rose nodded. "Well, I better get on home," she said reluctantly. "I have to go help my Mom get ready to leave for the funeral, but Dad said I could stay home by myself for a few days, so I was hoping that maybe you could come over."

"Oh, Rose, I just had the wildest idea! While your parents are out of town this weekend, we can go to the mall and a movie!" said Kristen excitedly. "It'll be so much fun!"

"I could not possibly do that," said Rose. "I would get in trouble if someone saw me."

"You won't look like Rose Mary Miller." said Kristen mysteriously.

Rose looked confused. "What do you mean?"

"I'll dress you in my clothes, do your hair, and put make-up on you."

Rose hesitated a moment but then agreed. "It could be our last girlhood adventure."

Kristen jumped up and hugged Rose, "Now don't you worry about a thing, I'll take care of all the details.

Chapter Three

Saturday had arrived and Rose could hardly contain her excitement as she hurriedly swept the kitchen floor. Kristen was due to arrive at any moment and today was their big day. Dad, Mom, and Katie had left for the funeral yesterday and Rose could hardly wait to take advantage of her freedom.

Humming a happy tune, she shook out the rugs. Rose smiled as she thought about how perfectly everything had worked out. Dad had agreed to let her spend the night with cousin Rebecca and get someone else to do the farm chores for the weekend. She felt a momentary twinge of guilt remembering the lies she'd told her parents. "It is not like I am hurting anyone," said Rose as she tossed the rugs down. Besides this is my last chance to spend the day with my best friend." she reasoned the guilt away.

Moments later a knock sounded at the door. "Come in," called Rose putting the broom and dustpan in the closet.

Kristen entered all smiles. "I can't begin to tell you how excited I am!"

"Me, too. I feel like I am having a good dream and I hope I do not wake up." Rose laughed. "I am a little worried about facing your parents, though," she admitted.

"No need to worry," Kristen reassured. "They are out of town."

Rose sighed with relief, glad she was spared facing Mr. and Mrs. Nelson.

"Are you ready to go over to my house and get started?" asked Kristen.

"I just need to grab my overnight bag and I will be ready" said Rose.

"I want this to be the best weekend ever for you," said Kristen as they climbed the stairs to her room. "You deserve to have some fun and be pampered. You work so hard on the farm."

Rose smiled, but kept silent unsure how to respond. She was not accustomed to having anyone make such a fuss over her.

"Shall we do your hair first?" "You have such pretty hair; I've always wanted to do something with it!"

"Make me look as non-Amish as possible," said Rose as she watched Kristen plug in the curling iron. "What are you going to do?"

"I'm not going to tell you," answered Kristen turning Rose away from the mirror. "I want you to be surprised."

Kristen worked quickly and silently, combing, curling and stopping every now and then to stand back to survey her work. "Time for a little makeup," she announced, "then you can see."

"I can hardly wait, I am not used to having my hair down except for when I wash it."

"Do you ever wish you could dress different?" asked Kristen as she concentrated on putting on the finishing touches to Rose's makeup.

"Yes. My cousins in Pennsylvania are not nearly so strict. They are allowed to wear bright colors and shorter dresses."

"Are you ready to see?" asked Kristen turning Rose toward the mirror.

Rose gasped with delight, "I do not even look like me!"

Her honey colored hair was parted on one side, falling gracefully down past her waist, and big soft curls framed her face. Frosty eye shadow, a little blush and cherry lip-gloss, completed the look.

Kristen smiled enjoying Rose's delight. "What would you like to wear?" she asked, pulling Rose away from the mirror and over to her closet.

Rose looked around the huge closet. It was filled with brightly colored clothes. Dresses, shorts, shirts, skirts and jeans, not to mention the fifty pair of shoes. I do not know," she laughed. "I wear dresses everyday. I will let you tell me what to wear."

Kristen looked through the closet full of clothes. "How about this?" she asked, holding up a pink and white summer dress.

Rose slipped on the dress and twirled gaily in front of the mirror. "I have never worn anything this short," she stroked the soft material of the knee length dress. "My Mom always measures my dresses so that the hem is no more than eight inches off the floor!"

"That's a shame," said Kristen. You have such pretty slim legs to show off."

"You are the first person to see them. No one is allowed to show anything off. I am not even allowed to wear short-sleeved dresses in the summertime," said Rose.

"We do have one slight problem though, said Kristen slowly. You will have to shave your legs if you wear that dress."

Rose looked shocked. "Really? I have never heard of that."

Kristen laughed. "Sure, I do it all the time," she said holding out a tanned, clean-shaven leg for Rose to inspect.

Rose hesitated. "But what about under my arms?" she blushed with embarrassment.

"Don't be embarrassed," Kristen said, ushering Rose into the bathroom and giving her the shaving supplies and a detailed demonstration. "Be careful not to cut yourself," she said over her shoulder as she exited to give Rose the privacy she knew her friend would want.

Rose smiled as she followed Kristen's instructions nearly laughing out loud as she thought of how her sister Katie would react.

"All done," called Rose sometime later. "I love the way it feels," she said. "I feel dumb that I never knew about it. But I am sure we are not allowed to shave."

"That's ok," reassured Kristen. "What would you like to do first?'

"I do not care," answered Rose.

"Then let's go to the mall first." decided Kristen "You'll love it!"

Just then the doorbell sounded. "Anybody home?" a voice called out.

Kristen ran to the door. "Lane!" she cried. "What brings you home?"

"I had a chance to ride home with some of the guys for the weekend."

"Oh, I am sorry, I didn't know you had company," he apologized.

Kristen looked puzzled having momentarily forgotten about Rose. "Oh, yes," she said with a mischievous glint in her eye. "Lane, this is my friend Rose."

Lane smiled charmingly, liking what he saw. A beautiful girl with long hair and pretty blue eyes. There was something familiar about that shy sweet smile, he took a closer look.

Kristen and Rose giggled, exchanging secretive smiles.

"What's going on?" asked Lane suspiciously.

"Come on, Lane," laughed Kristen. "Don't you know who this is?"

Lane's mouth dropped open in surprise. "Rose!" You leave me speechless. I haven't seen you in like three years?"

Rose nodded. He was even more handsome than she had remembered.

Lane smiled showing two deep dimples. "You're going to have to fill me in on what's going on here." Experiencing the same weakness in her knees as she felt when she was thirteen, Rose blushed dropping her eyes at his smile.

Unable to contain herself Kristen burst forth with the entire story. "And now we are off to the mall," she finished. "You can come with us if you like."

Lane shook his head declining the invitation. "I have to do some work on the computer for Dad. Maybe we could meet later for dinner. Where are you going to eat?"

"I don't know yet," replied Kristen as they made their way out the door. "Call me on my cell later."

"I cannot believe you get to come here all the time!" said Rose after several hours of walking in the mall.

Kristen laughed. "I'm glad you like it, but my feet are killing me. Let's go find a place to sit down. The two girls soon found an empty bench next to a beautiful water fountain.

Rose looked down into the cool sparkling water. "What are all the pennies on the bottom for?" she asked curiously.

"People make a wish when they throw them in. It's for good luck." answered Kristen handing Rose a penny. "Go ahead try it."

Rose laughed. "Today I have everything I could wish for."

Kristen shook her head. "You are too much. You liked everything!"

"I have never experienced anything like this before," said Rose. "We usually go into one small store. I never knew that there were so many things to buy!"

"I should be more thankful for all that I have." said Kristen feeling humbled.

"It feels strange that no one is staring at me," commented Rose looking around. "I always feel so self-conscious when I go out in public."

Kristen nodded sympathetically. "People can be rude," she agreed. "I'm going to miss you so much Rose," sighed Kristen. "You always help me see life differently."

"I will miss you too," said Rose sadly.

"You'll have to write and tell me when you're ready to get married," said Kristen.

"I am twenty and I have never even had a date," said Rose.

"Is there someone you'd like to go on a date with?" asked Kristen curiously.

She thought about the boys in their small community, none of them appealed to her.

"How about my brother?" teased Kristen, remembering how Rose blushed when Lane smiled at her.

"Oh, Kristen he would never give me a second glance. I will admit though I have had a crush on him since I was thirteen," Rose said.

Just then Kristen's cell phone rang, interrupting the conversation.

"Hey, Lane," said Kristen. "We were just talking about you."

Rose shook her head threateningly, motioning her to keep silent.

Kristen grinned and chattered on. "Where do you want to eat?" she asked. "Sure that's fine. Ok. We'll see you there." "It's all set," said Kristen putting the phone back into her purse. "Lane said he'll meet us at the Pizza Palace in about a half hour."

The two girls made their way leisurely toward the exit, taking their time to browse through several more shops. "This has been so much fun!" said Rose as she got into the car. "I do not think I have ever enjoyed myself so much." Opening her bags, she checked over her purchases. She had decided on a beautiful stationary set with her birthday money from Grandma, and a box of chocolates, which were her weakness.

"Here is a little something from me," said Kristen handing her a bag.

"Oh, you shouldn't have!" said Rose setting the bag on the seat beside her.

"Aren't you going to see what I got you?" asked Kristen.

"I was not sure if I was supposed to open it now," admitted Rose. "I am not used to getting gifts for no reason."

Kristen nodded understandingly, reminded again of the simple life her friend led.

Reaching into the bag Rose cried with delight. "Oh, Kristen, I love it!" she said admiring the beautiful gift basket, filled with lotions, powders, soaps, body shampoos and perfumes. Rose looked over at Kristen. "You should not have done this you spent way too much money on me!"

"You're worth every penny," insisted Kristen pulling into the restaurant parking lot. "Come on, let's go in and see if Lane is here yet."

Rose followed Kristen into the restaurant. She could only remember two other times that she had eaten in a restaurant, and she was looking very forward to the experience.

Rose looked around the dimly lit room. Little round tables filled the center of the large room while cozy looking little booths lined the walls, and to complete the romantic atmosphere were soft love songs being played in the background while several couples swayed to the music on the dance floor. The girls spotted Lane in a corner booth and made their way over to his table.

Lane stood up smiling as the girls approached. "I saved this spot especially for you," he smiled flirtatiously at Rose, patting the seat beside him. "It's not every day I get to sit with such a pretty girl." Rose blushed hesitating to sit beside him.

"Never mind, Lane," Kristen spoke up."You know how he likes to tease."

"But I'm not teasing," smiled Lane looking at Rose.

"You better not be! I may still be able to beat you arm wrestling," said Rose feeling a bit more confident, recalling a summer day when Lane was sixteen and she was thirteen.

Lane laughed. "Oh, no! I hoped that you'd forgotten about that! I'll never hear the end of it will I?"

"I hope you ordered already. We're starving!" declared Kristen.

"Yes, I ordered a pizza." Lane replied.

"Sounds good to me," Both girls responded.

"So did you buy out all the stores?" asked Lane as they waited for the pizza to arrive.

Hardly," replied Kristen. "We didn't have enough money."

"We did have a great time though." said Rose enthusiastically. "I have never been to a mall before."

"You've got to be kidding," said Lane. Every girl he knew made it her second home. "Did you like it?" he asked knowing he would enjoy her answer.

"Oh, yes, it was great," Rose said.

Lane smiled. He enjoyed watching Rose. He liked the way her eyes lit up whenever she smiled. She is like a little girl on Christmas morning, he thought to himself. All this is totally new for her, he realized.

"Do you still ride Abby?" he asked remembering his time spent on the Miller farm.

"Yes, I do. Dad says she is getting too old, but I think she still has a lot of spunk left."

Lane laughed, thinking how very different Rose was from the kind of girls he was used to hanging out with.

"This is great," said Rose when the pizza arrived. "I could live like this every day!"

Kristen laughed. "Me too!" she agreed.

The three of them lingered over dinner, as they laughingly reminisced of days when they were carefree children playing on the Miller's farm.

"I cannot begin to tell you how much I enjoyed the day," said Rose for the third time as Kristen showed her to the guest bedroom. "I learned a lot about your life today, and it was so much fun. Even the shaving," she said laughing at herself. "Now I will not feel so dumb when my cousins talk about going out to eat and going shopping."

"Oh, Rose, you're not dumb! You've just led a very sheltered life. That's nothing to be ashamed of," said Kristen.

"I just wish I could have the opportunity to go away to college like you are doing. I wish I could choose to do what I want. Instead, I am expected to get married and have a big family. I know this may sound silly, but I have always dreamed of becoming a nurse," Rose confided.

"No, that doesn't sound silly," said Kristen. "At least you know what you want. I've been exposed to everything and I'm still not sure what I want to do."

"I wish I had not lied to my parents," said Rose regretfully.

"I'm sorry, too," agreed Kristen. "But I'm glad we got to spend the day together. Who knows when we will ever be able to do it again?"

Rose lay awake a long time after Kristen had gone to her room. She thought about all the things she had seen and experienced that day. What would it be like to live in a world where she could make her own choices? It was no use, she was Amish and to leave the community was unthinkable. If she left, she would be cut off from her family and shunned. She knew her parents believed that there was no hope of going to heaven if a person left the Amish church. Rose was not sure if she agreed with that idea quite as strongly as her parents. Is there even hope for me, Rose pondered. First she was in trouble for being angry with her father and now she had lied to her parents.

Unable to sleep, Rose crept quietly out of bed and made her way downstairs to the back deck. Sitting down on the top step, Rose breathed in the fragrant aroma of Mrs. Nelson's flower garden, the full moon, bathing everything in its silvery light. Rose sighed with contentment enjoying the sweet serenity.

"Having trouble sleeping?" asked a deep voice behind her.

Rose jumped, startled. "Hi, Lane, I am sorry I did not mean to wake you."

"It's ok," said Lane sitting down beside her. "I was up working on the computer."

"I could not sleep, so I thought I would come out here and enjoy the full moon," said Rose, feeling nervous at his nearness. "It makes everything look so beautiful."

"Not as beautiful as you," said Lane softly, reaching over to take her hand.

Rose smiled shyly her heartbeat accelerating at his gentle touch. "No one has ever told me that before," she said quietly.

"I wanted to tell you all evening," said Lane looking into her eyes. "I thought about asking you dance, just so I could hold you," he caressed her hands softly with his.

"I would have liked that," whispered Rose.

Taking her hand, Lane stood up and pulled her gently into his arms.

Rose felt the warm feeling in her heart spread through her body and down to her toes; her legs feeling too weak to hold her, she leaned against his chest. Tipping her face toward his, Lane lowered his head until their lips met in a sweet, lingering kiss. Rose returned the kiss, her arms crept around his neck, and she snuggled a bit closer. Lane felt his own heartbeat quicken at her sweet response. Pulling her closer still, he kissed her again. Rose loved the feel of his lips, strong and tender against her own. This was what it felt like to be loved her heart sang.

Lost in a world of passion, and wanting more, Lane swept her into his arms.

Longing to be loved, Rose gave herself to an intimacy with him known only to lovers.

Chapter Four

The cheerful chirping of bluebirds outside the window awakened her. Stretching contentedly in the big waterbed, Rose snuggled deeper under the cover of soft satin sheets. Slowly she opened her eyes and looked around the room, Lane's room. Suddenly memories of the previous hours came flooding back. Rose turned expecting to see Lane beside her, but only the sun's morning rays touched his pillow.

Rose quickly slipped out of bed and made her way to the guest bedroom, slipping on her dress and combing her hair. Her feet feeling like they barely touched the floor, she smiled at her reflection in the mirror. Lane loved her. She blushed as she remembered the sweet nothings he'd whispered in her ear and the soft kisses they'd shared. Anxious to find Lane, Rose hurried downstairs making her way to the kitchen, pausing when she overheard her name.

"What do you mean, you slept with Rose?" she heard Kristen ask indignantly.

"Exactly what I said," replied Lane calmly. "I slept with Rose."

"You are so arrogant, Lane Nelson!" cried Kristen. "You think you can have any girl you want! But let me tell you, Rose is not like your stupid friends!"

"I know she might be your best friend, but I'm not marrying some dumb Amish girl just because I slept with her one time!" he said carelessly.

Their eyes met across the room. Rose stood frozen unable to move. She felt as though the pain in her heart would take her breath away. Her eyes began to fill with tears; I must get away, she thought, and bolted for the door.

"Rose wait!" Lane called.

Rose kept running, she could not stop, she had to get away. She wanted to run; run away from the pain. She headed for the creek, her place of solace. Maybe there she could turn back the time, go back to twenty-four hours earlier when all she had to think about were her chores.

Rose cried until there were no more tears, she felt cold and empty inside. How could something that started out so beautiful have turned into something so horrible? She asked herself as she headed toward home. Last night she had felt so special, so loved. Now she felt dirty, and rejected. Could God forgive her for the sin she had committed? She had known better. Rose thought of her own father and his reaction when she was disobedient, surely God could not tolerate such a huge sin. God was holy and sinless. I have three more days until Dad and Mom come home, maybe by then I will be able to face them. She sighed; her feet felt heavy and tired. A great weight of guilt and shame settled upon her. Would she ever feel clean or free again?

"My, my! It sure looks nice in here!" exclaimed Mom upon her return from Pennsylvania. "It certainly looks like you've been busy while we were gone."

Rose smiled, glad Mom had noticed. She had thrown herself into her work the past three days, hoping she would be able to fall asleep more easily at night. She hated the long hours of tossing and turning miserably until sleep came. Her mind kept going over the weekend's events, wishing desperately she could erase it all.

"Wow, you even washed all the windows!" commented Katie.

"Ah, it is no big deal," shrugged Rose. "I had to have something to do."

"Work is good," said Dad. "Idle hands are the devil's workshop," he quoted.

Rose picked up Katie's suitcase and carried it upstairs. She wished that just for once Dad would have thanked her for taking care of things and for all the extra work she had done in his absence. Compliments were not a part of Dad's vocabulary, she concluded bitterly

Even though it was September, the afternoon sun felt scorching hot to Rose as she worked, picking basket after basket of tomatoes. The last of the garden, she thought thankfully. "I have come to join you," called Katie holding up a glass of water. "Want some help?"

"I sure would," agreed Rose downing the glass of water. "Thanks."

"I went to town for Mom this forenoon," said Katie a bit later as the two of them continued to work side by side. "And," she paused for effect. "I ran into cousin Rebecca."

Rose kept silent, praying her secret was safe. But her hopes were dashed at Katie's next words.

"You never did spend the night there did you?" she asked pausing in her work and looking sternly at Rose.

Rose shook her head feeling sick with guilt; her secret, or at least part of it, was out. "Do Dad and Mom know?"

Katie shook her head. "I did not tell them."

Rose felt relieved; she hated to think about the consequences if her father found out!

"Rose, why can't you behave? What did you do?" Katie asked.

"Something I should not have done."

"Oh, Rose, it is bad enough that you get into trouble with Dad, please do not get in trouble with the church, "said Katie turning back to her work.

Rose picked up another basket and began filling it with the last row of tomatoes. Yah, it would be bad to be in trouble with the church. If her secret came out she would be punished, be made to confess her sin before the entire congregation and be excommunicated and shunned. Rose shuddered at the thought, praying that her secret would never be revealed.

"Rose," called Mom from the bottom of the stairs. "Time to get up."

"Ok," mumbled Rose rolling over and pushing back the covers. Every part of her body ached and several waves of nausea washed over as she sat up and swung her legs over the edge of the bed. Feeling dizzy , Rose made her way to the window for a breath of fresh morning air. She laid her aching head gently on the windowsill waiting for the nausea to pass. "It would not do to be sick," she said to herself. Today she was going to help brother Joseph put up silage.

Moving slowly Rose got up and slipped on her dress and apron, knowing Mom wouldn't excuse her from her chores. Mom always said a person felt better to move around a bit even when sick, but by the time morning chores were finished Rose highly doubted that Mom knew what she was the talking about. The chores had seemed endless and she certainly felt worse now than she had before. Pouring warm water from the teakettle into the washbasin she prepared to wash up before breakfast.

"What is wrong?" asked Katie bringing a clean towel to hang on the rack.

"I think I have the flu," said Rose wiping her face and hands on the towel. "Please tell Mom I do not feel like eating breakfast."

"Ok, I will tell her," agreed Katie heading for the kitchen.

"Thanks," said Rose over her shoulder as she hurried outside to be sick. The smell of pancakes and sausage, were too much.

"Are you ok?" asked Mom coming out onto the porch several minutes later.

Rose shrugged. "I do not feel well." she mumbled.

"You do not look good," fussed Mom reaching over and laying her hand on Rose's forehead. "You are not running a fever," she diagnosed. "Is your tummy hurtin'?"

Rose nodded, suddenly feeling close to tears. It had been a long time since Mom had made such a fuss over her. She found herself wishing she were a little girl again, back to a time when Mom was able to soothe away all her hurts.

The next three days Rose spent lying in bed, with Mom, making teas, and offering various home remedies to ease the nausea and vomiting.

"If you are not better by morning, we will have to take you to see Doctor Smith," decided Mom, "in case it might be your appendix."

The next morning brought no change, so Mom made arrangements to take Rose to see the Doctor. "I will drop you off here, and then I will go down the street to get groceries," said Mom pulling the horse and buggy to a stop in front of the Doctor's office. "Are you ok to go in alone?"

Rose nodded. "Yah you go ahead I will be fine." Climbing off the buggy she bade her mother good-bye and headed inside. Unsure of what to do, she approached the receptionist. "Hello, I'm Rose Miller. I have an appointment with Dr. Smith."

"Ok, Honey," smiled the lady behind the counter. "Go ahead and have a seat and we'll call you shortly."

Rose hung up her coat and bonnet and took a seat. She wished she were back at home lying on the couch. She picked up a magazine hoping it would help pass the time, but overwhelmed with nausea she laid it aside.

The nurse soon called her name and ushered her into the exam room. Taking her vital signs, asking a few questions the nurse soon left her alone. Rose looked around the tiny room. The charts on the wall that had fascinated her as a little girl were still there. Rose took a deep breath and tried to relax. I hope I do not have to wait too long, she muttered to herself. I am sure they will think I am silly for coming in here for stomach flu.

A knock sounded at the door. "Good morning, Rose," smiled Dr. Smith.

Rose smiled back. He looked just like she remembered, tall and thin with glasses.

"You were just a little thing when you came in the last time. Did your arm heal ok?"

Rose nodded, remembering her last visit. She was nine years old and the cause of the visit was a broken arm that had occurred when she had fallen off her pony. "It is fine now," she answered twisting her hands nervously anxious for the exam to be over.

"What brings you here today?" he asked, taking a seat.

"I think I have the stomach flu, and I have pain here," she said laying her hand on her lower abdomen.

Dr. Smith put on his stethoscope and began the exam, stopping now and then to ask a question. "I'll send the nurse in to draw some blood and get a urine sample, and then we'll know for sure what's going on," he explained before leaving her alone once more.

Seconds later the nurse arrived, medical supplies in hand. Rose felt nervous as she watched her prepare to draw blood. What if it was serious after all, she worried. Why else would they go to all this bother?

Rose felt like an eternity had passed until Dr. Smith finally came back into the room. Pulling up his chair, Dr. Smith sat down, shuffled the papers in his hand, then folding his glasses he put them in his jacket pocket. "Are you married Rose?" he asked.

Rose shook her head.

"Do you have a boyfriend?" he questioned.

Again Rose shook her head, wondering why Dr. Smith was asking these strange questions. "Well, Rose, I don't know how else to tell you this," he paused. "You're pregnant."

Rose stared at Dr. Smith in shock. "Are you sure?" she whispered at last. A million thoughts were racing through her mind. What would she do? What would her parents say? Rose covered her face with her handkerchief and wept.

Dr. Smith looked with compassion at the young girl before him. He knew Rose came from a strict Amish family. In all his years of serving the Amish, he had never encountered this.

The next several moments were a blur to Rose as she tried to concentrate on the doctor's instructions. "Here are some things that will help you," he said putting some reading materials in her hand. "And a bottle of prenatal vitamins, make sure you take one every day," he instructed.

"When is my baby due?" her voice came out in a strange whisper.

"Well, according to the information you gave me, I estimate it to be May 15," he said thumbing through the little calendar on his desk.

Rose gathered her stuff and stood up to leave. "Please do not tell my parents," she begged.

Dr. Smith nodded. "If there is anything you need, please don't hesitate to call."

Rose paid her bill and stepped out into the bright sunshine, relieved that Mom was not there waiting. She made her way over to the bench and sat down. She would have to compose herself before Mom returned.

Fear, now mingled with the guilt and shame that weighed upon her as Rose faced the reality of knowing that it would be impossible to keep her secret forever.

Chapter Five

The sound of a horse and buggy approaching brought Rose back to the present. Slipping on her bonnet, and tying it under her chin, she hurried to meet her mother.

"What did the Doctor say?" Mom asked as Rose settled down on the seat beside her.

"Uh, he said it was just the flu," Rose lied, avoiding eye contact with Mom. She felt sick at the pit of her stomach. When would all the lies stop? Her list of sins loomed before her.

"You are just going to have to take it easy for a couple days until you get your strength back," said Mom. "Katie can help Dad until you are up and about again."

Rose nodded but did not answer.

The two rode in silence. Rose was glad Mom was not in her usual talkative mood. She needed time to think and sort things out. Oh if only she would have said no! The moment had been so special, being held and told she was beautiful. Was it really possible for a guy to say all those things just to get a girl in bed, but not really mean them? She asked herself, angry that she had fallen for Lane's sweet talk.

Rose tried to block it from her mind as she listened to the rhythmic clip clop of the horse's hooves as they made their way through the small winding county roads, roads that were lined with towering age-old oaks and maples clothed in their glorious, fall splendor, Rose watched the brightly colored gold and red leaves fall lazily to the ground. But the beauty of the cloudless azure sky and bright autumn colors went unnoticed as the question played itself over in her mind: What am I going to do?

In the weeks that followed, Rose hid her morning sickness from her family. Breakfast was most difficult, it took every bit of strength she had to remain seated at the table and force down a plate of Mom's scrambled eggs. She had read every pamphlet that Dr. Smith had given her in the privacy of her room and from the information she'd gathered, Rose knew her morning sickness would soon be over.

"Being sick really wasn't the worst part," thought Rose one evening as she made her way back to her favorite spot by the creek. It was the feeling of guilt and fear that plagued her every night as she lay in bed waiting for sleep to come.

Out of habit, Rose walked over to the hidden mailbox in the old oak tree to check for a letter from Kristen. She gasped with delight when her fingers felt the little envelope that had been hidden inside. There was a letter!

She quickly found a seat on a log and began reading.

> Dear Rose,
> I'm sorry it's taken me so long to write. First of all I want to apologize for Lane and how he hurt you. I'm so ashamed of my brother! I haven't spoken to him since. I'm sorry I couldn't find you that day. I came back to the creek but you weren't there. I can't imagine the pain you must be feeling. I'm so sorry. Please let me know that you are ok. Did your parents ever find out what we did? I hope not!

I miss the country. I'm still not used to city life. I've been insanely busy with classes and working. I was home over the weekend for Aunt Marge's funeral. I wanted so much to come see you but I knew that wouldn't be wise, so I wrote this letter instead. Please let me know how you are doing.

Love ya,
Kristen

Rose wiped away her tears as she finished the letter. She had enclosed a stamped envelope for Rose knowing it would be difficult for her to get one without her Mother's permission.

She thought back to that awful Sunday morning when she had run from the Nelson's house back to the creek. Knowing Kristen would come to look for her, Rose had waded up the creek and onto her brother's property. She had not wanted to face anyone, even her best friend.

Folding the letter, Rose stuck it in her coat pocket. What should she write? She certainly could not tell Kristen about the baby! Rose picked up a rock and tossed it into the creek. She shivered as the cold November wind blew through her thin coat. "I had best get back to the house before anyone notices I am missing," she decided, heading toward home.

The sound of the howling wind outside her bedroom window caused Rose to pull the warm quilts tighter around her wishing she could just stay in bed. Her body ached from yet another sleepless night. Rose slipped out of bed and hurried to get dressed. Today was the Miller's turn to host a church service in their home.

The past several weeks had been spent cleaning every nook and cranny of the Miller's old farmhouse. The walls were washed down, the windows cleaned, and the floors polished until they shone.

"Well I think we're ready," Mom said as she set the teakettle on the woodstove after breakfast. "You girls go ahead and change your clothes before folks start comin'. You know Annabelle is bound to be early, she likes *nix so feil* as to try and catch us not yet ready."

Rose hurried up the stairs to her room. She looked longingly at her bed. Having gotten up at four, nearly five hours ago already, she felt tired at the thought of the long day still ahead of her.

"Maybe I will wear my new dress today," Rose thought as she peered into her closet at her meager wardrobe. She thought back to all the dresses that had hung in Kristen's closet, making the seven dresses in her own small closet seem pitiful. "Four good dresses for Sunday wear is enough," Mom had told her when Rose had wished for more. *Ah Vel* maybe Dad and Mom were too poor to buy more; she thought as she took out her navy blue dress and slipped it on. Next came the white organdy cape and apron, Rose carefully pinned them in place and checked her reflection in the mirror. Noticing that her apron needed tightening, she pinned it again, this time a bit tighter. The five pounds she'd lost made her look thin. But not for long, thought Rose anxiously laying her hand on her stomach.

Just then a knock sounded at her door. "Come in, called Rose taking a quick look around the room making sure everything was neatly in place.

"Hi Rose," greeted cousin Rebecca. "I had a chance to come a bit early this morning."

"That is nice. It has been a couple weeks since I last saw you." said Rose.

"Yes, I missed you in church, Katie said you were sick. You look like you've lost weight?"

"A little," Rose admitted wanting to change the subject. Even though she and Rebecca had always been good friends, Rose could not bring herself to confide her deep dark secret to Rebecca.

"I was hoping to have a chance to speak to you privately today," said Rebecca taking a seat on the bed.

Rose's heart sank. "Oh, no here it comes!" she moaned silently. "Why is that?" she asked.

The usually confident Rebecca seemed a bit nervous herself. "I, uh, just wanted to tell you that I had my first date last Sunday," she blushed.

Rose held back a huge sigh of relief. "Oh Rebecca! Who was it? Are you in love? Tell me!"

"It was Norman Byler. I don't know if I am in love yet, but thinking about him makes me happy."

Rose smiled, hardly believing what she was hearing from the ever sensible Rebecca. Soon several more girls joined them, and the subject of Rebecca's love life was dropped.

"Time to come take your seats," Mom called up the stairs.

The girls formed a line starting with the oldest girl first and made their way down stairs, taking their place with the women in the kitchen. They took their seats on backless wooden benches that Rose and Katie had set up the night before. The living room too had been emptied of furniture and then filled with the same wooden benches for the men and boys.

The men and boys soon filed in behind Bishop Dan, and several hymns were sung to begin the service, next the preaching, and lastly the closing hymn. At the close of the last hymn, Rose got up and stretched. She had had a hard time keeping her mind on Bishop Dan's preaching. She had been so tired it was hard to stay awake. It felt good to get up and move around a bit, even if it did mean getting lunch for all the people, thought Rose as she helped set up the benches into makeshift tables.

The tables were covered with tablecloths, and the traditional Sunday lunch was served. There were large platters of thick sliced homemade bread, butter, jam, pickles, beets, and mixed peanut butter. The peanut butter was mixed with corn syrup and marshmallow fluff to spreading consistency, a favorite with everyone. For dessert, there was tea, coffee, and cookies of all kinds.

Rose looked around the room at all the familiar faces, aunts, uncles, cousins and neighbors. Everyone was laughing and talking, getting caught up on the events of the past week. "What would life be like away from all this?" wondered Rose. Here in her world, everyone knew everyone and everything about one another. "Except for me," thought Rose. "No one knows my secret."

"You're awfully quiet today," said Lena. "Are you feeling better?"

Rose smiled; glad to see her oldest sister. "Hi Lena. I am ok, just tired. We have been working pretty hard getting the house cleaned for church today."

Lena nodded understandingly. "I am sorry I could not come help, but with a three week old baby I am afraid I wouldn't be very much help."

"That is ok, I know you have your hands full," thinking of Lena's big family, this recent addition making number ten. "Where is baby Jonas?" asked Rose.

"Ruby is taking care of him, they like playing Mom." laughed Lena.

"I can only imagine," Rose laughed. "Is he a good baby?"

"Oh, yes, very content. The only thing I have to do is feed him. Everyone fusses over him so! Why he hardly has a chance to cry!" smiled Lena.

"It is nice your girls are big enough to help you." commented Rose.

"Yah it is." agreed Lena. "Speaking of help, I was wondering if you could help out some friends of ours? Their names are Michael and Michelle Bennett. She was in an accident this past week and lost her leg. Michael was wondering if we knew of someone who could come and stay the winter."

"You will have to ask Dad," said Rose.

"I know they are not Amish," continued Lena, "but they are good people, we have known them for years. Sometimes, they are taxi drivers for the Amish in emergencies."

A feeling of excitement grew within Rose as she listened to Lena's request. This would was the opportunity she'd been longing for, a chance to experience life outside the community.

The rest of the day Rose was kept too busy to think about Lena's proposal. There was food to serve, dishes to wash, and the usual daily farm chores to be done. But at last the day was over. Rose trudged slowly up the stairs to her room, her feet aching with every step.

Rose smiled as she thought back over her conversation with cousin Rebecca. Rebecca had been unusually happy and talkative all day. She was most of all relieved that Rebecca had not brought up her failure to appear at their house that Saturday evening in August.

Rose leaned over and blew out the flame in her little bedside lamp. Tomorrow she would find out if Dad would let her go work outside the community.

Chapter Six

"Can you spare Rose for this winter?" Dad asked Mom the next morning as they sat down for breakfast.

Rose held her breath as she waited for Mom's answer. "Surely they can make it without me, fall cleaning and corn husking are done."

"I reckon I could. We are pretty well caught up with the work. Katie can help me with winter sewing."

"We could use the money," said Dad leaning back in his chair. "But I hate to send Rose into the world." He stared out the window. "Lena says they are good people and help out the Amish too."

Rose waited anxiously for Dad's verdict. She wished she could beg like Katie would. But Rose knew it would not make any difference in Dad's final decision.

"Yah we sure could use the money, Mom agreed. Things are tight in the winter."

"Well, I reckon it is decided then," Dad said.

Rose could hardly contain her excitement the rest of breakfast she was finally going to see what living outside the community was really like.

It was later that afternoon when Rose finally put the last piece of clothing in her suitcase and snapped it shut. She took one last look around the room, making sure she had not forgotten anything.

"That is it," she said aloud. "I am ready."

"Rose your ride is here," Katie called up the stairs.

Grabbing her suitcase Rose hurried down the stairs.

"You shall mind our rules!" warned Dad sternly. "Make sure you come home to attend church."

"Yah I will," promised Rose.

With several quick last minute instructions Rose was out the door to meet Michael Bennett.

"Hi, you must be Rose," said Michael extending his hand in a friendly manner.

"Yes," answered Rose, feeling nervous around this strange man as she returned the handshake.

Michael took her suitcase and, and opened the passenger side door for Rose.

"Thank you so much for agreeing to do this," said Michael taking his seat behind the wheel.

"I am glad I can help," said Rose politely.

"We have four children," Michael continued, "and they are excited to meet you."

"What are their names?" asked Rose.

"Melissa is six, the twins, Jordan and Jaden are three, and baby Kayla is seven weeks old. So you see I have my hands full with my wife being laid up."

"Is she home from the hospital yet?" inquired Rose.

"No, my Mother is staying with us right now. She has to leave tomorrow. That is why we wanted you to come today, this way Mother could help you get acquainted with all there is to do."

"That is good," said Rose, feeling relieved. She had been worried about what she was going to do with all the modern appliances. Not having grown up with electricity, these things were foreign to her.

Rose soon found she need not have worried. Michael's Mother was a sweet lady and took Rose under her wing and showing her how to operate each appliance, making a list of all the chores to be done.

"Here is my number," said Mrs. Bennett the next day as she prepared to leave. "If you have any questions, please call me."

Rose suddenly felt very alone as she watched Mrs. Bennett's car leave the driveway. "Whatever am I going to do?" she asked herself. "I hope I will be able to handle this on my own."

A cry from the nursery brought the twins running. "The baby's crying! The baby's crying!" both boys chimed in at once running up to Rose.

"I think she's hungry," said Rose as she took both boys and led the way into the nursery.

"Can I hold her?" asked Jaden.

"Can I give her the bottle?" asked Jordan.

"Sure. You can both help," laughed Rose as she took baby Kayla from the crib. "You're alright now, baby," Rose reassured. "The boys and I will take good care of you."

Both boys followed closely behind her as she led the way back into the kitchen.

Placing the water into the microwave, Rose stared at the panel of buttons. "I can't remember how to do this," she groaned, pressing a series of buttons, only to hear a loud beep.

"I know! I know!" Jaden said. "Let me do it. I know which button to push. First you push this button," he demonstrated. "Then this button." A small whirring sound started and the microwave was on.

Rose laughed in spite of herself. "You are a very smart boy Jaden."

The two boys soon lost interest and went back to their games leaving Rose alone with her thoughts. She looked down at the tiny infant in her arms. "Soon I will have a tiny baby like this too," Rose felt a stirring deep inside her. "What will my baby look like? Maybe she will have my blue eyes and Lane's dark hair," she said to herself, picturing a tiny infant with soft pink skin.

"What will I do?" she felt panic rise up within her. "More importantly what will Dad and Mom say? It will be several more weeks before I have to tell them," decided Rose as she rocked baby Kayla.

Rose loved the big soft rocker and everything else in the Bennett's nicely furnished living room. There were big over-stuffed chairs and sofas, thick carpets, long floral drapes, and best of all were the family pictures adorning the walls.

Rose felt a twinge of guilt for enjoying the luxury of all the modern conveniences around her. "What was wrong with upholstered furniture, or carpet?" Rose wondered. "Did it make one a better person to do without it? Must be not," she concluded, it certainly didn't seem to help her be able to obey her parents any better.

"Rose, where are you?" a small voice called from the kitchen.

"I am in here," answered Rose softly.

"Hi," smiled Melissa as she ran into the room and kicked off her shoes. "May I hold her?"

"Sure, come sit on the other rocker then you can finish giving her the bottle."

"I am a big helper," said Melissa proudly, as Rose placed the baby in her arms.

"That's right," agreed Rose smiling. "Maybe you can help me make supper."

"I used to set the table for Mommy," Melissa informed her. "Now I will have to help Mommy a lot since she has only one leg." She finished sadly.

Rose felt a pang of sadness too. "What could she say to comfort the little girl?"

"I learned a new bible verse in school today," said Melissa as she rocked back and forth. "Shall I say it for you?"

"Yes I would like to hear it."

"It goes like this," chattered Melissa pausing a moment in her rocking. "*Casting all your cares upon Him, for He cares for you.* 2 Peter 5:7.

"That's very good," praised Rose.

"*He cares for you*," the line kept going through Rose's mind as she went about fixing supper. "Could God forgive someone who had committed such a terrible sin?" she wondered. "Especially someone who knew better? Why can't I be like Katie? She doesn't rebel at the rules or get in trouble. Dad never yells at her," she thought as she washed up the last of the dishes. "Certainly God loved people like Katie, but probably she was a trial to God, just like she was to her father." She concluded hopelessly.

Chapter Seven

Two weeks had passed and the big day was finally here! Today, Michelle was coming home from the hospital. Rose had gotten up early to clean the house and do the laundry. She wanted to make sure everything was perfect for Michelle's home coming.

"I hope she likes me," worried Rose as she went back through each room double checking to make sure it was clean.

"The house looks great," complimented Michael coming into the kitchen to get a cup of coffee. "Michelle will be so pleased."

Rose smiled her thanks. "Is there any special food I should make for her?"

"I'll see if they have special instructions for her diet, but I think she will be able to have whatever she's hungry for." replied Michael. "Do we need any groceries?" he asked.

"Well there are a few things we are out of. I could make a list," offered Rose.

"That'd be great," answered Michael. "I'll be ready to leave in about fifteen minutes, if you can have it ready by then."

Taking a pen and notepad, Rose looked in the fridge to see what was needed. She smiled to herself as she made the list: milk, eggs, bread. These items were never on her Mother's grocery list. Growing up on a farm they always had their own milk and eggs. Mother would never think of buying bread. She prided herself in always providing homemade bread for her family. It was what any good self-respecting Amish woman would do.

"Yes, life was definitely easier at the Bennett's," decided Rose as she thought about how quickly she'd gotten used to using the washer and dryer and even the microwave.

Thinking about her family, she experienced a pang of homesickness. Mom and Katie were probably at a quilting bee or apple shnitzing. Winter was the time the womenfolk got together and shared their work, and got caught up on all the latest news. Yah, it would be nice to hear from home again, she thought longingly.

"The church people will be bringing meals in starting tomorrow night, they will probably do it for the next week or so," Michael said as he took the grocery list from the table.

"Oh, that's nice," said Rose. Maybe people weren't so different outside the community after all, she thought. Her own people were always doing things like that too.

Rose looked at the clock. It was almost 3:30. Michael was due to arrive home at any moment with Michelle. "It's time for Mommy to come home," said Rose calling the twins. "Let's wash your faces so you will look real nice."

"Will Mommy bring us anything?" asked the boys bounding into the bathroom.

"We will have to wait and see," said Rose as she scrubbed their little faces.

"I wuv you!" said Jaden reaching out and giving her a big hug. "I am going to hug Mommy too."

"Daddy said Mommy will need lots of hugs," put in Jordan.

"Yes that is right," she agreed returning the hug affectionately. She had quickly grown to love the Bennetts' children.

Rose thought back to the evening before and the conversation she'd overheard Michael having with his children, while she'd been washing the supper dishes.

"Mommy is coming home tomorrow," Michael announced to the children. "I want you all to be good for Mommy. Ok?"

Rose had to smile as she remembered the children's enthusiastic response.

"We'll be super good Daddy!" Melissa had said. "Yes, yes, super good," the twins had agreed.

Then the conversation had taken a serious note as Michael continued. "Do you remember when Mommy had her accident?"

"Yes," they all agreed huddling closer to Michael.

"Mommy hurt her leg real bad, right Daddy?" asked Jordan his little face serious.

"That's right," agreed Michael. "Mommy's leg was broken and hurt too bad to fix," his voice getting husky with emotion as he tried to hold back the tears. "The doctors at the hospital made a new plastic leg for Mommy."

"Can Mommy still walk?" asked Jaden sounding scared.

"Yes Mommy can walk with crutches," answered Michael.

"Will she have to use the crutches forever?" asked Jordan.

"No, not forever, just for a little while." reassured Michael.

"Why did such a bad thing happen to Mommy?" Melissa cried. "Weren't there any angels watching over Mommy?"

Rose had stopped in the middle of wiping down the counter, tears springing to her eyes as she too waited for Michael's answer to his little girls' question.

"I don't know why this happened to Mommy," answered Michael after a short pause. "But I know there were angels there. Jesus tells us in the bible that he will never leave us or forsake us. If Jesus hadn't been watching over Mommy, she could have been killed."

Rose had finished with the dishes deep in thought. How she wished she could have such conversations with her father! Every morning Dad read them a portion of scripture, but he never talked about God. Rose felt herself drawn to the openness with which this family talked about God. They talked about God as if they knew him personally.

The sound of the front door opening brought Rose quickly back to the present.

"We're home!" called Michael from the kitchen.

Both boys raced toward the kitchen. "Mommy! Mommy! They cried. "You're home!"

Rose stayed in the shadows of the living room, watching the happy reunion. Michelle was tall and slender with shoulder length black hair. Her dark brown eyes filled with tears as she slowly bent down to hug her little ones.

Staying close by her side Michael kept an arm of support around Michelle, his own eyes brimming with tears of joy at having his family together once more.

Feeling like an intruder, Rose slipped quietly into the nursery to check on baby Kayla, who lay in her bed cooing happily. Rose smiled down at her. "You know Mommy is home, don't you? Shall we see if your diaper needs changing before Mommy holds you?"

"Rose where are you?" called Melissa. "Mommy is here. Come see her."

"Ok," answered Rose, Picking up baby Kayla and heading for the kitchen.

Michelle smiled at Rose through her tears. "You must be Rose. Thank you so much for coming. Oh there is baby Kayla!" she cried. "Michael, would you please help me sit down and hold her?"

Taking his wife gently by the arm, Michael helped her into the rocking chair. Rose handed over baby Kayla and soon the entire family was gathered around Michelle.

"I just can't tell you how grateful I am to be home!" said Michelle looking around at her little family. "God is so good isn't he?"

Leaving the family to get reacquainted on their own, Rose headed out to the kitchen to start supper. She felt overwhelmed with emotion, at Michelle's kindness. She loved the way the Bennett's were so tender and loving with one another.

Opening the refrigerator, Rose began to take out the ingredients needed to make supper. She was going to try and give them the best home cooked meal they ever had.

A tired sigh escaped her lips as Rose climbed the stairs to her room. "It was a good tired though," she thought to herself as she prepared for bed. Michelle had thanked and complimented her for the wonderfully clean house, and the fantastic supper. Rose smiled; glad she had gone the extra mile to make it the best supper possible. There had been baked chicken, scalloped potatoes, creamed peas, homemade bread and Michelle's favorite dessert, carrot cake.

She definitely got tired easier than she used to Rose realized as she prepared for bed. Stepping in front of the full-length mirror, Rose pulled her nightgown snuggly over her stomach, choking back a feeling of panic as she gazed at her swelling abdomen. Slowly she ran her hand over it. Can it really be that a real baby is growing inside me?

Going over to her dresser Rose took out the pamphlets from Doctor Smith. According to her calculations she was fourteen weeks along in her pregnancy. Running her finger down the list she read the progress development for week fourteen.

Your baby is now approximately three and one half inches long, Rose read aloud, and weighs one and one half ounces. Your baby's hair is beginning to grow and has now probably even begun to suck its thumb.

Just then, Rose felt a flutter of movements in her stomach. It was real! Rose placed both hands on her swollen abdomen. This was her baby, her and Lane's. Rose thought about Lane, she felt herself recoil at the thought of his reaction toward the baby. He would very likely blame her for trying to trap him! No he must never find out, she decided. This was her baby. Rose felt an overwhelming rush of love for the life within her. This was her baby and no one could take it away.

She thought about Dad and Mom as she crawled into bed. Soon, very soon, she was going to have to face them. She wouldn't be able to hide her growing secret much longer.

Chapter Eight

"It sure feels good in here!" exclaimed Rose coming into the kitchen and setting down her suitcase.

"Yah it does," agreed Mom. "This is the coldest winter we had in a good long while."

"I think so too." agreed Rose.

"Dad and Katie are just finishing up the milking," said Mom bustling around the wood stove as she hurried to finish supper. Katie will be glad to see you, I think she gets lonely when you are gone."

"I miss her too," said Rose as she hung up her coat and bonnet. "What shall I do to help?"

"You can set the table and cut the bread. Katie made it fresh this morning." Mom said as she took the fried pork she had prepared, and placed it on the back of the wood stove.

"It smells *gute* in here," said Rose hungrily, suddenly realizing how much she missed Mom's good home cooking. Mom didn't comment but kept on fussing over the meal she was preparing.

Rose thought about how quickly she'd gotten used to the nice compliments she received at the Bennett's, Mom however, wasn't used to them, she was the perfect example of the Amish women of the community with her long navy dress that brushed the tops of her shoes as she walked, and her clean white apron tied neatly around her slightly plump waist. She certainty couldn't picture Mom ever using a microwave. Rose almost giggled aloud at the very thought.

"Rose watch what you're doing!" came Mom's sharp rebuke.

Rose jumped, startled. So deep in thought she had failed to notice that the water picture she was filling was overflowing.

"Sorry," said Rose feeling silly. Grabbing a towel, she quickly wiped up her mess.

The back door flung open and Katie breezed in bringing with her a blast of cold air. "That wind is strong!" she said slamming the door behind her. "You are home Rose. Did you just get here?"

"A couple minutes ago. Are the chores done?"

"Yah, Dad will be right in, he is just closing the chicken coop."

"Let's make quick, and get the food on the table girls, so Dad doesn't have to wait." Mom instructed.

The girls hurried to set the steaming hot bowls of food on the table, and quickly took their places.

Rose felt her body tense as Dad stepped into the kitchen. She was glad she was seated behind the table. Right now her stomach felt huge, she felt like she had a sign on her forehead with the words: 'I am pregnant.' Rose swallowed nervously, her face feeling hot. Surely Dad would not suspect she was hiding something? Do not be silly; she scolded herself, no one knows.

Dad came and took his place at the table and everyone bowed their heads for a silent prayer, giving thanks for the meal. Rose thought how different the atmosphere was at the Bennett's, with Michael laughing and talking with his children as they shared their meals. She wished it were that way in her home.

"Could you pass the bread?" Katie asked, nudging her.

"Uh, yeah sure," answered Rose grabbing a piece of the warm fresh bread before passing it on. She ate heartily enjoying the fresh pork and potato soup.

"The soup is *gute*, Mom," complimented Rose. "You make the best soup."

Dad paused in his eating and looked at Rose. "Is that what you are learning from those outsiders?" he demanded.

Rose felt her stomach tie up in knots. "I – I don't know, I mean no."

"That is the way of the world, telling each other how great they are and soon they are filled with pride," he spat contemptuously.

Rose looked down at her plate. "I'm sorry," she said her voice barely a whisper.

The remainder of the meal was eaten in silence. Rose wished she could run upstairs and cry the tears that pushed at her eyelids, but knowing that would not be permissible she stayed, struggling to get the now tasteless food passed the lump in her throat.

"We lost our best horse to colic this week, and that is why Dad is so grouchy," Katie whispered to Rose as the two of them washed the supper dishes.

Rose nodded but did not answer. "Michelle lost her leg, but I have not seen her treat anyone badly," she wanted to say. "Dad always uses his bad moods to manipulate everyone into treading lightly around him," she thought with disgust. "It is not fair!"

"Do you want to play checkers?" asked Katie once the dishes were done.

"Sure, I will play," agreed Rose with more enthusiasm than she felt. What she really wanted was to escape to the privacy of her room, but knowing she wouldn't be permitted to do so until bedtime prayers were said, Rose settled down to an evening of checkers with her little sister.

"I think you are losing your touch," teased Katie after her third win in a row.

"No you are just stealing all my good moves," accused Rose laughingly. She wished she could be strong like Katie and not let Dad's bad moods affect her. It seemed that more often than not his moods were directed at her.

"Rose, Katie, time to get up," Mom called.

"Oh no," Rose groaned. It surely cannot be time to get up." Five a.m. now felt like three a.m. after getting to sleep until seven every morning at the Bennett's. Rose rubbed the sleep from her eyes and forced herself to leave the comfort of her warm bed. She shivered as her feet touched the floor. The old hardwood floor felt like ice. There is nothing quite as cold as an upstairs bedroom in an old farmhouse, Rose decided, as she hurried to put on her barn clothes. She knew Dad would be out there and started, and it would not do to dally around and get another scolding.

The familiar smell of hay and silage permeated her nostrils as she entered the barn. Did you come to greet me?" asked Rose, as Seven came bounding toward her, tail wagging. "You missed me didn't you?"

Grabbing a milk pail, Rose prepared to begin the milking. "Whoa Daisy," she patted the small black and white cow. Taking her position beside the cow, she began milking. The first sounds of the milk streaming into the bottom of the stainless steel bucket, alerted the cats of the pending meal. They came quickly, some of them with new families in tow. Rose laughed as she watched them. "Nothing ever changes around here," she said aloud.

"And that is the way it will remain," Dad said as he brought her a fresh bucket, so she could continue with the milking.

Rose groaned, somehow she had done it again.

"Be sure and dress extra warm this morning," Mom advised, as Rose made her way up the stairs to get dressed for Sunday church services.

"I will definitely need an extra pair of socks," she said to herself. The eight-mile ride to Uncle Joe's, in these sub zero temperatures, were enough to get severe frostbite if one wasn't careful.

Rose sighed disparagingly, it was her second attempt to pin the front of her dress neatly over her now ample bosom. "I am glad I can wear a cape over all this, she muttered. Hopefully it will help hide it." Taking a step back she surveyed herself in the mirror, there was no hiding the small tale-tell bulge in her midsection. Taking a deep breath Rose tried to suck in her stomach. "Ah it is just no use," she moaned. She would have to be careful to stay in the background, she decided.

The three-hour long service began and Rose determined that today she would focus on Bishop Dan's message. Maybe in it, she would find the answer to her dilemma.

The slow tune hymn singing came to a close and Bishop Dan took his place before the congregation. "Dearly beloved brothers and sisters in Christ, how grateful I am to have the opportunity to get together with all of you. However today is a sad day for us all."

Rose looked around the room, noticing the majority of the congregation was dressed in black. Everyone was extra sober, some of the people were weeping openly. What was going on? Rose wondered. Had someone died? No one had mentioned anything to her.

Bishop Dan continued. "One of our own has been deceived. Many shall be deceived in the last days," he quoted. This erring brother has been studying the Bible and fellowshipping with those outside the community. He has become so proud as to confess that he knows he is saved. He says he is certain he will go to heaven when he dies. Oh let us be wary of the pitfalls of pride!" He cried. "Surely we are in the last days when many are being deceived."

People were nodding in agreement with their leader. Rose sighed, certainly she would have to face this too; the disapproval of her people, once they found out. The thought made her feel sick at the pit of her stomach.

"This wayward brother has chosen to take the vows he made at baptism, and forsake them! He has chosen to go out into the world. The bible clearly tells us that we are to stay in that which we were brought up in." He thumped his Bible, to punctuate his words.

Rose listened as Bishop Dan continued to warn the congregation to watch for wolves in sheep's clothing, and how the road to heaven was very narrow, with only a few traveling on it. "There is only one thing left to do, to show our last love to this poor lost brother. He will be excommunicated and shunned. We will do this according to scripture, and give such a one over to Satan that his soul may be saved in the day of Jesus Christ," he concluded, quoting 1Corinthians 5:5.

The remainder of the service held the same somber tone, leaving Rose depressed and hopeless.

"Hi Rose," greeted cousin Rebecca after the service. "Did you freeze on your ride over this morning?"

"Almost," answered Rose, giving a mock shiver. "My feet are still cold!"

"How do you like your new job?"

"I like it, the Bennett's are very nice."

"Well just be careful," admonished Rebecca. "After all we heard here today from Bishop Dan, one cannot be too careful when talking to outsiders."

Rose wanted to defend the Bennett's, but knowing that would not be wise she remained silent hoping Rebecca would change the subject.

"They haven't tried to get you to study the Bible with them have they?" asked Rebecca.

"No, they haven't. How are things with you and Norman?" asked Rose changing the subject.

"He has asked me to be his steady girl," she smiled proudly.

"Congratulations. Maybe soon you will be telling me of your wedding plans?"

"Probably next year this time," grinned Rebecca unashamedly. "I am twenty already! I do not want to end up an old maid!"

Rose nodded, the stigma of *old maid,* being shameful among all the young girls.

She sighed, with the added shame of having a child out of wedlock, it was certain to be her lot in life.

Chapter Nine

Grabbing both baskets and balancing one on top of the other, Rose headed for the laundry room. It was Monday forenoon and she was happy to be back at the Bennett's. She thought about Katie at home helping Mom with the weekly laundry. Doing laundry at home was definitely a much harder job. It required getting up at five a.m. and filling the big black kettle with water that was pumped by hand from the washhouse pump. Mom would then start the fire under the kettle and begin sorting the laundry. Rose had the job of getting the little cakes of homemade soap, cut up into little squares and melting it in a small copper pot on the wood stove. The whites were boiled, and scrubbed clean on the washboard. Laundry was to hung on the line by seven a.m. so as not to be out done by a neighbor. Though no one ever said as much, Rose long felt, that was the case.

Rose grinned as she set the dial on *hot water*, and prepared to wash a load of whites. "I could get used to this real easy."

"Did you have a nice weekend?" asked Michelle as Rose began to prepare lunch.

"I guess." She had been glad to see Mom and Katie, but Dad, well that was an entirely different story. Then there had been church, and that too had turned out to be very depressing.

Michelle wished she knew what was going on with Rose. She was always so willing to serve. She couldn't shake the feeling that something was going on with Rose. But what was it, and how could she help her? "Dear Lord, please help me to show Rose how much you love her." she breathed a silent prayer.

"I know you don't know me very well yet, but I'd like to be your friend. If you ever need to talk, I'm here for you," offered Michelle.

"Thank you," said Rose swallowing back the sudden rush of tears. "Ah what is wrong with me today anyhow!" she scolded herself, resolving to better hide her emotions.

"We are having a small group Bible study tomorrow evening and I was wondering if you would make a dessert for us to enjoy afterwards?" asked Michelle.

"I like making desserts," said Rose. "What would you like me to make?"

"How about some sticky buns? asked Michelle. "Anything you make will be good."

"I'm sorry I was so gloomy this morning," Rose apologized later that afternoon as she helped Michelle fold the laundry.

"That's ok, I have those days too, at certain times of the month." Michelle said reassuringly.

"No, it is not that," said Rose.

"If it's something you want to talk about, I'm here for you."

"It's my dad, I can't ever seem to please him," Rose sighed and preceded to confide in her new friend what life with her father was like.

Michelle listened sympathetically, "I'm sorry; but I do know that I know you have a heavenly Father who does love you very much. You do know that right?"

"Rose shrugged. "I don't know how he could. I am not *good* enough. And, uh, I have done some very bad things." She blurted out.

"We have all done bad things, Rose." The Bible says in Romans 3:23 *all have sinned.* That is why we need Jesus.

"But what about doing something really bad that cannot be undone?" asked Rose anxiously.

"I think my favorite verse is in 1 John 1: 9" Michelle said, opening up her Bible. "*If we confess our sins, He is faithful and just to forgive us and cleanse us from all unrighteousness.*" She read.

"I don't remember hearing that verse before," Rose replied.

"If you want I could pray with you," said Michelle.

"I guess," said Rose hesitantly, not sure if she should even be talking to Michelle after Bishop Dan's admonishment yesterday about talking to outsiders.

Reaching over to take her hand Michelle prayed.

> "Dear Heavenly Father,
> Please help Rose to know how much you love her and how special she is to you. Your word says that we shall know the truth and the truth shall set us free. I pray, Father, that you would help Rose to find the truth. In Jesus name I pray. Amen."

The truth shall set you free, the line kept playing itself over in her mind as Rose got ready for bed that evening. "What could be better than being free?" she asked herself.

Her mind went back to the day she'd been baptized. After several months of meeting with the Bishop and ministers to be instructed in the rules and traditions of the Amish ways, she was taken in as a member and baptized. She had gotten down on her knees before the entire congregation and renounced Satan and the world, promising to remain a member of the Amish church and abide by all its rules for as long as she lived. Bishop Dan then sprinkled water on her head and baptized her in the name of the Father, the Son and the Holy Spirit.

Rose remembered how good she had felt that day. Mom had taught her that baptism washed away all ones sins."But what about now?" she despaired.

There was only one thing to do, she decided as she got on her knees beside her bed. She would ask the God of heaven who knows all things, to reveal to her the truth and set her free from this horrible weight of guilt.

"What do Amish people believe?" Michelle asked her husband as he crawled into bed that night.

"You mean spiritually?"

"Yes," answered Michelle, recounting that afternoon's conversation with Rose.

"I have tried to talk to several of the men but they are pretty tight lipped about their beliefs. One of them did tell me that they don't believe you can know whether or not you are going to heaven. He said everyone will stand before God and be judged according to their deeds."

Michelle shook her head sadly. "No wonder Rose worries about whether or not God can forgive her."

"Lets pray for her shall we?" suggested Michael taking his wife's hand.

Together they went before the thrown of the heavenly Father asking Him to show Rose how much He loved her.

Chapter Ten

"May I stir it please?" begged Jaden dragging his chair over to the kitchen sink.

"Yes, just let me get you a spoon," said Rose as she helped him situate his chair.

Rose smiled, reminded her of her own little nieces and nephews when they came over. It was especially nice having them around because of the positive affect they had on her father. If there was one thing that made her usually stern father smile it was his grandchildren.

Just then Michelle hobbled into the kitchen. "Oh these crutches make me so tired," she groaned sinking into the rocking chair Michael had specially placed in the kitchen for her.

"I'm helping Rose make sticky buns," announced Jaden proudly.

"Me too," echoed Jordan, climbing up onto the counter top.

"Did Rose say that was ok?" inquired Michelle.

Jaden nodded. "She said I could stir it," he answered waving his spoon for her to see.

"You'll have to tell me how to make them. I never learned how to do that kind of stuff at home," said Michelle regretfully. "My mother worked and she didn't like to cook, so we either ate out or had TV dinners."

"I would think that would have been fun." commented Rose as she brought the sugary syrup to a boil.

"Sometimes it was fun," admitted Michelle. "But we also got tired of it. You are very fortunate to have learned so much about cooking and baking. When I got married, the only dish I knew how to make was macaroni and cheese."

Rose laughed, finding that hard to imagine. "I have had to help in the kitchen ever since I can remember, and in the barn for that matter," she added.

"How old were you when your mother taught you how to start baking?" asked Michelle curiously.

"Well I don't know exactly," Rose said, "But I was nine years old when I made my first cake by myself. It was Katie's birthday and I wanted to surprise her. I begged Mom to let me make the cake. Mom finally agreed, and gave me a recipe to follow. I looked at the ingredients; it was just a plain old white cake. I wanted it to be special, so I decided to add a few things. I looked through the cupboards and found a box of jello, and a bag of cinnamon candies that were left over from some sugar cookies Mom had made for church lunch. Well I don't remember what all I added, but we could not eat the cake." she laughed.

Michelle laughed too, "You have come a long way then, because everything you've made since you've been here has been delicious!"

"Thank you," said Rose having learned that that was the proper response to a compliment. "I enjoy baking. I have to help outside with farm work so much that I don't get the chance to as often as I would like."

"Well I am sure you will make some guy very happy," teased Michelle. "The way to a man's heart is through his stomach you know."

Rose forced a laugh. At this point, it is the only thing I'll have to offer, she thought dismally.

As Rose laid in bed, she thought back over the Bible study and how confident everyone seemed of God's love and forgiveness. In fact, the Pastor said God was waiting to forgive. Unable to sleep, Rose crept quietly down stairs, desperate for answers. Maybe the answers were in the list of scripture references Pastor Ron had passed out on forgiveness. Making her way into the living room, she switched on the small reading lamp beside the sofa.

"There it is," she said, spotting the list lying on top of Michelle's open Bible.

Flipping through the Bible until she found the first reference, *For you Lord are good and ready to forgive and abundant in mercy to all those who call upon you.* Psalms 86:5. Rose read.

"I saw the light out here when I put Kayla back in her bed. Is everything ok Rose?" asked Michelle.

Rose shook her head, the lump in her throat preventing her from speaking.

Michelle made her way to the sofa and sat down. "Would you like to talk about it?"

Rose nodded helpless to know how or where to start.

"Have you ever asked Jesus to come into your heart and wash away your sins?" asked Michelle.

"Yes, once when I was about ten or eleven."

"What happened?" asked Michelle curiously noticing Rose's hesitation.

"I was at my cousin's house and I read a book about this little girl who had done something bad, then later in the book she prayed and asked Jesus to forgive her and to come into her heart. After she finished praying, she felt a wonderful feeling of peace. And from that day forward she was a very good little girl."

Michelle nodded. "I think I read that same book."

Rose continued. "After I went home, I went up to my room and prayed that same prayer, but nothing happened.

I was so disappointed. I was definitely not a nicer girl from that day on. "I have often wondered why it worked that way for her, and not for me?" questioned Rose.

"It takes faith to be born again," Michelle said. "Do you believe that God can forgive your sins?"

Rose nodded. "When I was baptized my Mom told me that all my sins were washed away on that day, but I have committed more and worse sins since that day," she confessed.

"We can be washed clean everyday by the blood of Jesus," Michelle explained. "In Hebrews 10:10 the Bible tells us that Jesus died once for *all* sins. All we have to do is repent and confess."

"Repenting is not so hard," Rose said. "But I don't know if I can ever confess, I am too scared."

"Why don't you first pray and confess to God, then ask Jesus to come into your heart." Michelle suggested.

Rose got on her knees beside the sofa.

"Dear Heavenly Father,

I confess that I have committed some very terrible sins. Please forgive me. And dear Lord Jesus please come into my heart, and wash away my sins and make me clean, Amen."

This was the second time Rose had prayed this prayer, this time she felt a sweet reassurance that God had heard and answered her prayer.

"Isn't God wonderful," smiled Michelle dabbing at her tears.

The two sat in silence each lost in their own thoughts.

"Remember when I told you I had done some bad things?" asked Rose.

Michelle nodded. "Would you like to tell me about it?"

"I am afraid you will think I am a very… uh… bad kind of girl," Rose twisted her hands nervously in her lap.

"I think I know what you're talking about," said Michelle. "I made the same mistake when I was your age."

"But you don't understand," whispered Rose. "I am pregnant!"

Holding back her gasp of shock and surprise, Michelle reached over and placed an arm around Rose, allowing her to cry on her shoulder.

Rose felt as if a huge weight had been lifted as she sobbed out her story to Michelle's listening ears.

"Does he know?" asked Michelle.

Rose shook her head, "I don't want him to know."

Michelle nodded understandingly. Knowing there were far greater issues to be taken care of at the moment. "Have you seen a doctor?"

"Once, that was when I found out I was pregnant."

"How far along are you?"

"I think I am about eighteen weeks." answered Rose.

"Are you taking vitamins?" asked Michelle.

"I was, but I ran out."

"Have you felt the baby move yet?"

"Yes, little flutters almost every day."

"Do you want to keep the baby?"

"Yes I do," said Rose.

"I'll get you to the Doctor and get you some vitamins and make sure everything is ok," reassured Michelle.

" I cannot do that," said Rose. "I do not have any money."

"That's ok," said Michelle, she had suspected as much. Mr. Miller had asked them to send the checks made payable to him. "Don't worry about it, we are sisters now. That's what family is for."

Chapter Eleven

Opening her suitcase, Rose began to unpack her few belongings into her own familiar closet at home. It was Christmas Eve and she was going to be at home for the next ten days to share the holidays with her family. She thought back over the past forenoon, making cookies and candy with Mom and Katie, in preparation for the next afternoon's festivities. After Christmas morning church services, all the relatives and families would get together and play games, sing songs, and exchange gifts. Knowing that confessing to Dad and Mom still lie ahead of her, Rose was having a hard time getting into the Christmas spirit.

"Why are you so quiet?" Katie had asked.

"I'm not quiet," Rose had forced a laugh. "I am just working hard."

It had been nearly two weeks ago that she had shared her secret with Michelle, she thought as she finished unpacking. She definitely felt better being able tell someone she realized, although the hardest part was going to be confessing her secret to her parents. Rose groaned at the thought of it.

"Oh Lord, please help me have the courage to face Dad and Mom," she prayed. She felt her stomach tie up in knots as she thought about her father's reaction.

"It is from the word of God that we get our strength and courage," Michelle taught Rose encouraging her to memorize scriptures.

Rose sat down and pulled out the little bible Michelle had given her. "I better get some strength now, she thought, because the first chance I get I am going to tell Dad and Mom my secret and get it over with."

"Now is my chance," Rose thought as she heard Katie entering her bedroom and closing the door. They had just said their bedtime prayers together and Rose and Katie had retired to their respective rooms for the night.

Rose listened, she could hear Mom's rocker creaking gently on the hardwood floor. "Probably doing a little reading," she guessed. "It's now or never," she decided.

Shivering partly because of her cold room, but mostly from fear, Rose slipped on her coat. Spotting the little Bible Michelle had given her; she slipped it in her coat pocket hoping its presence would give her the courage she needed. "Please be with me Jesus and give me courage," she prayed as she made her way down the stairs.

Rose cleared her throat nervously as she entered the living room. "I uh, I need to talk to you."

Both parents looked up from their reading. "Is everything ok?" asked Mom.

"I wanted to confess that I lied to you last summer. I didn't go to Rebecca's house when you went to Pennsylvania, like I said I was going to."

"You lied to us?" asked Dad anger in his tone.

"Yes, and I am sorry."

"Is that all you've been lying to us about?" he asked suspiciously.

Rose shook her head. "I uh, I did something bad," she said her voice barely above a whisper. "And now I am pregnant."

For two whole seconds there was complete silence in the room, and then Dad was on his feet grabbing for the belt, coming toward her. In that moment Rose relived every time Dad had whipped her. The time she had dropped a gallon jar of milk and it had spilled all over Dad's Sunday shoes, and for the time she forgot to shut the calf pen and they had escaped, running all over the neighborhood. The list went on.

Rose knew what to do; she closed her eyes and steeled herself against the blows she knew were coming. As the blows landed, stingingly across her face and backside, Rose grabbed blindly for the doorway to steady herself.

"Who were you with?" he demanded his voice filled with rage.

Rose trembled afraid to answer, causing more blows to be delivered.

"Was it a boy of our own community?"

Rose shook her head.

"Was it an outsider?" he asked outraged.

This time Rose nodded.

"You have shamed us and are no longer worthy to be a daughter!" he spat as he delivered several stinging slaps across her face. "I want you out of my house you - you harlot!"

"No! Eli, please," pleaded Mom getting up from her rocker. "Its too cold."

"Be still and sit down," Eli ordered his wife.

Mom sank back into her chair sobbing, covering her face with her handkerchief.

Grabbing Rose by the shoulder, Dad shoved her out the door.

Rose stumbled and fell into the snow, scrambling to get to her feet she ran out the lane, and down the road fleeing into the darkness.

Rose kept running, more than anything she wanted to distance herself from the awfulness of what had just occurred. Her breath came in giant gasping sobs, fear welled up inside her. Where was she going to go? For a brief moment, she thought about her sister Lena, maybe Lena could take her in. Lena has her hands full already; Rose crossed the option off her list. Asking a family member for help would just cause problems. Everyone would have to side with Father. He was upholding the laws of the church, shunning the errant.

Sinking down beside the road to catch her breath, Rose sent up a silent prayer asking God to help her. She looked out across the snow covered valley at a handful of farms tucked in against the hillsides, most of them belonging to her brothers' and one to her sister Esther. Only great Grandma Kauffman's house had a lamp still burning in her window. Probably up with her arthritis, figured Rose wondering if she would ever see Grandma again.

"I need to keep moving before I freeze," she shivered, anxious to put some distance between her and her father. Her hands numb with cold she put them on her face to cool the sting of her Father's blows. Blood trickled through her fingers, where the delicate skin on her lips and cheeks were broken. Rose scooped up a handful of snow and held it on her face and nose to stop the bleeding. Bowing her head to ward off the cold north wind, she got up and began walking. I need a plan Jesus, she prayed. Please Help me. Help me know where to go and what to do.

Coming in view of the Nelson's she looked longing at their picturesque home, Christmas lights decorating every tree in the lawn, and little candles flickering invitingly in each window. "Oh if only she could talk to Kristen! But that would mean facing Lane. Fierce pride welled up within her. She would not be "dumb" a second time. Being rejected once was more than enough.

The Bennett's needed her, she said to herself and even though, it would take awhile to walk there she knew she could do it she thought determinedly, wrapping her coat a little tighter around her she quickened her pace.

Rose was glad for the cover of darkness as she passed Roman Hershberger's farm, his wife, Annabelle being a notorious gossip, would certainly have a field day with the current events in the Miller family. Rose knew her family was always under scrutiny with her father's position as deacon.

The headlights of a car broke through the darkness, coming straight toward her. "Please don't stop," she muttered walking a bit faster only to have the car roll to a stop several feet in front of her.

"Is everything ok?" asked the elderly gentleman rolling down his window.

"I uh yes," answered Rose keeping her head bowed in hopes of hiding her bruised and bloody face.

"If you need a ride somewhere honey, we can take you," offered the sweet grandmotherly lady from the passenger seat. "It's too cold to be out tonight."

"Oh thank you but I can walk," Rose declined. "It's not that far."

"Well you shouldn't be out on a cold night like this with just a coat." said the elderly gentleman. Opening his door, he reached in the backseat and grabbed a blanket. "Here take this," he insisted, holding out the blanket. Rose tucked her chin as she reached for the blanket, but the garish yellow glow of his interior car lights quickly played across her bowed head and exposed what Rose was trying to hide. The kind Samaritan quickly came to her side. "What happened to you?" he asked.

"I would rather not talk about it," requested Rose. "I am sorry."

"Oh please don't apologize," he said putting the blanket around her and steering her back toward the car. "Please let my wife fix ya up." Helping her into the backseat, he quickly ordered his wife to bring the first aid kit from the trunk.

The little grandmother gently and tenderly cleaned the wounds. "You really should see, a doctor," she said. "That eye looks pretty bad."

"I'll be fine," Rose said. "Thank you so much," she wiped at her tears. "You are so kind."

"We are going to our son's for Christmas and we would love to have you join us," invited the sweet little lady.

"Oh no, that's ok, you have done more than enough already," Rose declined the invitation.

"Well then take these," she said placing several candy bars in her hand along with their card. "Our number is on the card, so if you change your mind or if you ever need anything please let us know."

Thanking them Rose slipped the card in her coat pocket along with the candy. "I will," she promised.

"Put these on too," the man insisted handing her a pair of gloves and a scarf, before leaving.

"Thank you Jesus," prayed Rose as she continued on her way, feeling grateful toward the old couple. Or could it be they were angels in disguise? Michelle said angels were everywhere. Maybe this was God's way of letting her know she wasn't alone.

Chapter Twelve

Rose stopped and rubbed her back. She looked around wishing she could find a spot to sit down and rub her sore feet. How long could it take to walk seven miles anyway? She groaned having no idea what time it was, or how far she'd walked. The moon was full and the air was crisp and cold, so cold it nearly hurt her lungs to take a deep breath. "At least it's not windy," Rose thought gratefully.

Rose walked on feeling more exhausted with each step. It had been a good long while since she'd passed a house, she realized, feeling lonely. A dog howled in the distance, sending a chill up her spine. "I hope he is not hungry," she thought fearfully remembering stories she'd heard about packs of wild dogs attacking humans. She tried to pick up her pace but the road seemed to stretch endlessly before her.

Rose rubbed her hands together to try and warm them. Her feet felt numb, she wished she could quit walking and give up. Tears rolled down her cheeks as her heart cried out to God. "Please help me. Rescue me! I can't do this anymore."

The snow squeaked beneath her feet as she walked. "One more turn and I'll be there," Rose kept saying to herself. "I can do all things through Christ who strengthens me," she quoted. The verse bringing her comfort, she repeated it again.

At last, she reached the front porch of the Bennett's home. She made her way up the steps, wishing she could just slip in quietly without waking anyone. She tried the door, but it was bolted securely. With no other options Rose took a hold of the knocker and banged it gently several times, then waited.

"Who is it?" Michael called out moments later snapping on the porch light.

"It's me Rose." Her voice came out barely louder than a whisper.

"Rose!" Michael exclaimed with surprise taking her arm and helping her inside.

"I am so sorry to bother you," Rose began. The warmth of the room making her feel dizzy. "I hope…." The rest of her sentence was lost as she fumbled for the chair in front of her just before everything went black.

"Do you think she'll be ok Michael?" Michelle asked worriedly looking at Roses' swollen and bruised face.

"I don't know," he answered sharing his wife's concern. "She looks pretty bad."

"What do you suppose happened to her?"

Rose stirred and tried to sit up. "I am so sorry," she mumbled.

"Are you ok?" they both asked at once, relieved to see that she seemed to be coming around.

"I'm cold," she whispered.

"I'll go get the electric blanket," Michael offered.

Moments later, he was back with the blanket and left Michelle to tuck her in, offering to go make a pot of tea.

"Thank you," Rose whispered and closed her eyes again.

"What happened?" Michelle asked after her husband left the room, knowing Rose would be more comfortable to talk when it was just the two of them.

"I told my parents and Dad got angry," she shuddered pointing to her face. "He said I was no longer worthy to be his daughter." She sobbed.

"There, there," Michelle reached out and comforted Rose much like she would her own six year old daughter.

Michelle could hardly believe what she was seeing and hearing. She had always thought the Amish were a pretty tight knit group. Were they not always helping each other out? And what about how the families forgave the man who shot and killed their innocent little daughters? What kind of guy was Eli Miller? She fumed, trying not to let her anger show. "

"How did you get here?" Michelle's questions came tumbling out.

"It was around bedtime when I told them," Rose began her story, telling Michelle about the old couple and how they had been so kind.

"It's a wonder you didn't freeze walking all this way!" exclaimed Michelle. "Certainly, God watched over you."

"Yes he did," agreed Rose thankfully.

"I think she should see a doctor, I'm afraid for her and the baby." declared Michelle to her husband as the two of them went back to bed.

"Yes certainly," agreed Michael.

"I'll call my cousin, Alex, maybe he could come and check on her," said Michelle

"We had a rather unusual experience last night," said Charles as he and his wife as they took their place at the breakfast table with his son and family.

"What happened Grandpa?" asked Kristen settling down for one of Grandpa Nelson's stories. She loved hearing his stories for as long as she could remember, the way his blue eyes would twinkle mischievously when he would stop at the best part, keeping her in suspense.

"Well about a half mile before we got here, we thought we saw someone walking-

"Walking in this weather?" interrupted Lane.

"Yes the poor thing, all she had on was a thin coat," Grandpa continued. "I stopped the car and asked her if she was ok, but she kept her distance and kinda kept looking at the ground. She assured us she was fine, but I just had a gut feeling something wasn't right."

"What did you do?" asked Kristen impatiently when Grandpa paused for a moment.

"Well we offered her a ride and she refused, so we gave her a blanket we had in the backseat. When I opened the door to give it to her, well that's when I saw her face."

"Did you know her?" asked Mrs. Nelson caught up in the story.

"No," he shook his head. "She was a young Amish girl, but someone had apparently beat her quite badly."

Kristen gasped. "What did she look like?"

"Well now it's hard to say really," put in Grandma. "I did get her to let me tend to the wounds on her face. She really should have had medical attention. I told her as much, but she reassured me she was fine."

"What did she look like?" Kristen repeated her question, afraid she already knew.

"Well she was probably about your height dear, and she had blue eyes," continued Grandma. "Such pretty blue eyes too. And what a sweet girl, she apologized for being a bother."

"What color hair did she have?" asked Kristen, now on a desperate mission to get the bottom of who the mystery girl was hoping desperately it wasn't Rose.

"Well she had on that white thing, I believe it's called a covering." said Grandma trying to remember. "I think she had light colored hair, blonde maybe? Why dear? Do you know this girl?"

Bursting into tears, Kristen ran from the room.

"What's wrong with her?" Grandpa asked. "Shall I go talk to her?"

"She thinks it might be her friend Rose," answered Mrs. Nelson pushing her chair away from the table to go after her daughter.

"I'll go Mother," offered Lane excusing himself and heading for the stairs.

"Mind if I come in? asked Lane sticking his head inside Kristen's bedroom.

"Why, what do you want?" asked Kristen angrily.

"I just came up to see what I could do?"

"Why? What do you care?" Kristen glared at Lane. "You are the one that broke her heart! She was a sweet, pure, innocent girl until you came along and ruined it all!"

Lane cringed at his sister's harsh words. "I didn't force myself on her, she was willing." He defended himself.

"You are so full of yourself. Just admit it, you took advantage of her."

Lane shrugged. "Whatever. You're making way to big a deal out of this. How does someone beating Rose equal up to me getting yelled at? Besides who would want to hurt Rose?"

"Her father." answered Kristen having one more than one occasion overheard Mr. Miller's harsh words.

"Why?" Lane questioned. "What could she have done-

"Wait" Kristen interrupted. "Is it possible Lane that she could be - well you know?" She couldn't bring herself to say it out loud.

"No, it was one night." Lane shoved his hands in his pockets.

"Lane there's a girl out there that might be carrying your baby!" Kristen stood up and grabbed his arm. "I know that fighting a war has changed you, but the Lane I used to know would care about something like that."

"Ok but let's not jump to any conclusions. There are lots of Amish families around here, and they all have at least dozen kids, there has got to be tons of girls that fit grandma's description."

"Lane Nelson, you owe it to me, and to yourself to make sure," Kristen demanded.

"Ok, ok. But just keep your mouth shut until we know for sure."

"So does that mean you'll help me find her?" asked Kristen.

"Do I even have a choice?" Lane asked.

"Thanks Lane. See, you don't have to be a soldier with me."

Mom wiped furiously at her tears trying to hold them in check. She knew her husband would be displeased if he saw them. "Oh why did he have to have such a temper anyway? And Rose who knows what has become of her?" Wiping her eyes with her apron she prepared to make breakfast. "It sure don't feel like Christmas anymore," she said setting the little pot of oatmeal on the stove.

"What was she to tell Katie? Katie was bound to ask, as were the people. How would they react? Certainly Rose would be shunned," she shuddered at the thought. But what had happened to Rose? Her mother's heart cried within her to know if her daughter was ok.

"Where is Rose this morning?" asked Katie coming into the kitchen. "Mom are you ok?" she asked seeing her tears.

Mom shook her head, not knowing if she dare speak of it. It wouldn't do to have her husband come in and catch her. "Where is Dad?" she asked in a hushed voice.

"He is harnessing the horse and getting the buggy ready for church."

"Rose got herself in trouble," Mom said sadly. "She told us last night she is expecting, and Dad told her she had to leave."

Katie gasped, speechless. How could this have happened? She never knew Rose even had a love interest, or a date for that matter. She knew several boys had asked Rose out in the past, but Rose being shy, had turned them down.

"Or at least that is what I thought," Katie said to herself. These and a million other thoughts and questions were racing through her mind.

"Did she say," Katie stopped in mid sentence hearing Dad's footsteps.

The two of them hurried to set breakfast on the table, a meal neither of them was hungry for.

Rose opened her eyes, momentarily confused until memories of the night before came flooding back. "No wonder my head hurts," she groaned, being careful to move slowly. "It's Christmas," she whispered. Christmas had always been her favorite holiday. She loved Christmas church. There were big bowls of candy on every table. It was the one-day the children were allowed to eat as much candy as they liked, remembered Rose fondly, wondering sadly if she would ever be part of it again.

Tears of regret trickled down her cheeks. Regret for sleeping with Lane, regret for bringing shame to her family. Would she ever enjoy a Christmas with them again? She thought about her thirteenth Christmas and remembering her disappointment when her gift was a hand painted picture and eight glasses. Oh sure it was pretty, Aunt Kathryn had specially hand painted it. But she was hoping for a board game, she admitted to her older sister Esther.

"Rose this is for your hope chest!" explained Esther who was happily courting the boy of her dreams. "Mom began getting me things for my hope chest too when I was thirteen."

Esther had been right, every year after that her gifts were things to be stored in her hope chest. Rose felt a deep sense of regret as she thought about the old cedar chest up in the attic, filled with embroidered pillow cases, crocheted doilies, and dishes. Marriage was out of the question, she realized. No Amish boy would marry a girl like me.

Rose thought about Mom and Katie who at this very moment would be gathering with the people at Mose Stoltzfus' for the Christmas service. The whispers would start when they greeted one another. Rose isn't here. Something isn't right, they would murmur their suspicions. Cousin Rebecca would demand Katie tell her what was going on, after all Rose was her best friend.

Rose knew Mom and Katie would not tell anyone today, But soon Bishop Dan would demand an explanation and then the people would find out. "Poor Eli and Mattie, what a disappointment to have a child turn out that way," the people would say.

"I am glad to have told them, even if it had to come to this," decided Rose. "I hope I never have another secret as long as I live." Exhausted Rose pulled the covers over her head and went back to sleep.

"Mom could you take a fruit basket over to the Miller's this afternoon?" begged Kristen.

"Why?"

"Well, tell them Merry Christmas, and then I will send a gift for Rose, and this way maybe I will know if Rose is, Oh please Mom I have to know."

Mrs. Nelson made her way up to the Miller's front porch with the gift, and fruit basket in hand. Setting the basket on the step, she knocked on the door.

Several seconds later, a stern Mr. Miller answered the door.

"We wanted to wish you a merry Christmas," she said handing him the basket.

"Thank you," he said politely making no move to invite her inside.

"Oh yes Kristen sent this for Rose," she said holding out the small gift bag.

At the mention of Rose, his face changed. "Tell Kristen to keep her gift," he said. "Rose no longer lives here," and with that said he closed the door, leaving a speechless Mrs. Nelson on the steps alone.

"It was very awkward," said Mrs. Nelson. "He seemed angry."

"I know he is very harsh with Rose," Kristen said.

"So you think it was Rose that our grandparents took care of last night? How can we find her? Would any of her family even talk to you?" asked Lane.

"I don't know but we have to find her," Kristen's eyes met Lane's in an unspoken message. Worried that what had started as her and Rose's innocent girlhood adventure, may have turned into something that was now costing Rose her family.

Chapter Thirteen

"Oh Alex, thank you so much for coming by," Michelle greeted her cousin several hours later.

"That's quite alright." Alex smiled. "I don't get to see enough of you and Michael anyhow."

"Did you bring the girls?" asked Michael referring to Alex's two young daughters.

"No. Grandma is keeping them. I have to go check a few patients at the hospital this morning too."

"How are you doing?" Michelle asked, thinking about the rough time Alex had gone through losing his wife to a brain tumor nearly two years before.

"Some days are better than others. Shall we go see the patient?" Alex looked at Michelle.

"Sure, she's right in here," she said leading the way to the downstairs guest bedroom. "I'll go in first and wake her."

"Rose, I need you to wake up."

"Ok," she mumbled sleepily.

"I asked my cousin Alex who is a doctor to come and make sure that you are ok." Michelle said gently.

"Oh no, you should not have!" protested Rose trying to sit up and get out of bed. "I am supposed to be here to take care of you."

"You're not trying to run away from me are you?" teased Alex coming into the room, trying to put Rose at ease.

"I'm Alex," he said shaking her hand. "Michelle tells me you had a rough time of it and we just want to make sure you are ok."

"I am ok," she insisted.

"I'm the doctor," smiled Alex. "How about I decide that."

"I know how I feel," muttered Rose. "It's not necessary to make all this fuss. All I need is some rest and I'll be fine."

"I'm glad to see you still have some spunk left," Alex said as he put on his stethoscope.

Michelle assisted Alex in gently removing Rose's garments to dress her wounds, holding back a sob when she saw the bruises across her back and legs that had quite obviously come from a belt.

Quickly and efficiently, Alex completed the check up and assured Rose her baby was fine. "You are severely dehydrated, and I'm afraid you will have to be admitted to the hospital and put on I.V."

"I can't. Please." Tears filled her eyes. "I will drink lots of water. I will do whatever you tell me to." she looked pleadingly into Alex's green eyes. "I can take care of myself," she insisted. "I don't want to be a burden to Michelle."

"I'll see what I can do," he promised. "I will bring something to treat that frostbite too. In the meantime just get plenty of rest."

"Thank you so much, I will," she promised.

"I'll be back later and get her started on an I.V.," Alex said as he followed Michelle back to the kitchen.

"Have you ever seen anything so terrible?" Michelle asked in disbelief.

"Someone should press charges!" he said angrily. "What kind of guys has this poor girl had the misfortune of growing up with?" Alex shook his head. "These are the kind of situations that make me feel helpless, because she needs so much more than just medical attention right now."

Michelle nodded in agreement. "Only God can heal those wounds."

"I see you have some color back in your cheeks, Rose," Alex smiled several days later as he completed his routine checkup. "Blood pressures better too," he commented, removing the cuff.

"I feel so much better," she smiled. "I think I will be able to start working again by tomorrow."

"How do you feel in here?" asked Alex thumping his chest.

"A little better. Michelle has been helping me with that," she said.

"Forgiving isn't easy but it is the only way to get healed on the inside. If you ever need anything, let me know," said Alex preparing to leave, sorry that his services would no longer be needed. He had come to enjoy this part of his routine.

"Thank you so much. I don't know when I will be able to pay you for all this." Rose apologized

"You don't owe me anything," Alex reassured. "What are friends for?"

"I do not deserve your kindness," said Rose. "Everyone has been so kind to me, and I feel bad because I have been a burden to Michelle and this whole thing is my fault," she said regretfully.

"Oh Rose don't say that," Alex sat down on the edge of the bed and took her hand. "This," he pointed toward her wounds, "is not your fault."

"If I just would not have gone…"

"Jesus washed all that away, when you received him as your Savior," Alex pointed out. "The bible even says: 'he remembers our sin no more.' "

"It's just that, I feel so ashamed," she said.

"Jesus bore our shame on the cross too. It's when we aren't willing to repent that we should be ashamed." Alex replied.

"Thank you, Alex. Please let me know if I can ever do anything for you."

"Well Michelle tells me you are a wonderful cook," Alex smiled. "When you are feeling better, I would love to have one of those home cooked meals I've heard so much about."

"I certainly will," promised Rose.

Careful to follow doctor's orders, Rose slowly got back into her routine at the Bennett's,

"I will be glad when my face heals," Rose told Michelle. "This way it won't be a constant reminder, and I will be able to forget what happened."

"Do you think about it a lot?"

"Yes, I guess so. I keep wondering what to do. I never really thought about not being Amish. I mean sometimes I would wish I could trade places with Kristen, but I never thought I would leave."

"Do you think you could still go to heaven, if you dressed like me?" asked Michelle, having heard that many Amish believed they were the only ones who would be in heaven.

"Oh yes, I believe that I can, its just that it feels strange to - to suddenly feel like I have no place to belong, and no family."

"Well you are now a part of our family," smiled Michelle. "You have been a big blessing to us."

"I feel the same way about you," answered Rose appreciatively. "But I know you won't need me in another week or so. You are getting around so well."

"I would still need you at least two days a week," said Michelle. "But you are welcome to stay as long as you need to, in the meantime we will pray that God will work something out."

"Telephone for you, Rose" Michael called.

Drying her hands on the dishtowel, Rose went to the phone. "Who could it be?" she wondered. She didn't think anyone knew she was here.

Rose took the receiver hesitantly. "Hello?"

"Oh Katie! It's so nice to hear your voice!"

"Don't cry! I am ok. Tell Mom it is going to be ok."

Michelle felt tears gather in her own eyes as she listened to the one sided conversation. She couldn't imagine how hard it had been for Rose to lose her family, and change her way of life.

"Does dad know you are calling?" she heard Rose ask. "I did not think he would let you. I hope he does not find out. I don't want you to get in trouble for me."

"Yes I am doing ok. Yes the baby is fine. I saw a doctor and he said everything was ok."

There was a slight pause before Rose went on.

"Uh I am sorry but I don't want to tell anyone that right now."

Michelle guessed that Katie was asking who the father was. She respected Rose for having the courage to keep it to herself, and accepting the responsibility. Although she felt angry with Lane for the way he had taken advantage of Rose.

"I am due in May," Rose answered her sister's question rather hesitantly.

"That's ok I know you don't have much time. I understand. Tell Mom I love her," her voice broke in a sob. "I love you too, Katie. Goodbye." Rose tried to hold back the tears but failed. It had been so good to talk to Katie. This was the first time she had ever told Katie she loved her. Those kinds of emotions were not displayed in their home. She could not remember ever getting a hug from her father, and she had been a little girl probably about five or six when Mom last hugged her. She had fallen off the hay wagon and had the wind knocked out of her. Mom had quickly run over, picked her up and hugged her tightly. "You'll be ok," Mom had gently reassured her.

Rose wiped at her tears, trying to compose herself. "That was my sister Katie, she had to go to the store so Mom gave her some money to call me. Dad didn't know so she was afraid."

"It's ok to cry," Michelle said hugging her.

"I feel like that is all I do these days."

Chapter Fourteen

"I don't want to pry into your personal affairs Rose, but I couldn't help noticing that you've been wearing the same two dresses for the past couple weeks."

"It's all I have here," said Rose. "I had left one here and then I left with only the one I had on."

"I might even have some clothes that would fit you. It looks like you are about ready to start wearing some maternity clothes," suggested Michelle kindly.

"Are you sure you wouldn't mind?"

"Not at all, give me a hand we can get them now," said Michelle heading toward her bedroom.

Shutting off the iron and setting it aside, Rose eagerly followed Michelle into the bedroom.

"Why don't you try this one?" she said handing Rose the plainest of the dresses first. It was a cute navy dress with an empire waist and puffed sleeves. She suspected that Rose probably wasn't ready for anything too bright or colorful, having worn only dark colors all of her life.

Rose chose the privacy of the bathroom to change into the garment, and emerged several minutes later all smiles. "I feel like a princess," she said.

"I think you look like an angel," spoke up Melissa who had come to join them.

"Thank you," said Rose twirling in front of the mirror admiringly.

"Do you feel comfortable in it?" asked Michelle.

"It does feel kind of strange," admitted Rose. "But I like it a lot."

"I don't want you to feel like I'm trying to make you change anything."

"I know you would never do that," Rose said. She had developed a high regard for Michelle in the past several weeks. "I do have a question though," she said a moment later. "I have been thinking about the covering. Do you think the bible teaches that women have to have their heads covered?"

"I don't think that it's wrong to wear a covering," Michelle paused praying that God would give her wisdom to guide Rose correctly through His word. "If you want we can take a look at what the bible says about it. In the meantime I think you should pray and ask God to show you."

"It feels strange to be wearing a covering with this dress, but I also feel naked when I do not have it on. Does that make sense?" asked Rose.

"Yes, I understand that, you've worn it all your life."

"Well I would like to leave it off for tonight, if you could french braid my hair."

"Sure I would love too. I can even teach you how to do it if you want." offered Michelle.

"Wow!" she exclaimed as she watched Rose release her long golden hair from the confines of its bun. "I didn't know you had such long hair! Have you ever cut it?"

"Oh no, we are not allowed to ever cut our hair."

"I have never braided such long hair," said Michelle tying a ribbon on the end of Roses' braid.

"You look purty!" Jordan declared, giving Rose a big hug.

"You are very sweet," Rose returned the hug. "Tonight I will make your favorite supper."

"Oh goody," he clapped his hands. "We are having sloppy joes!"

"But I thought beans were your favorite?" Rose teased.

"No." Jordan's face fell. "I don't like beans."

"Ok," Rose grinned pinching his cheeks. "Sloppy joes it is."

"You look nice Rose," complimented Michael as everyone sat down at the dinner table. "What's the special occasion?"

"Women don't need special occasions to look nice dear," Michelle reminded him.

"You're right honey," Michael agreed. "I apologize Rose."

"No need to apologize," Rose reassured. "I do look much nicer in-."

A knock sounded at the front door interrupting her reply.

"Who could that be?" Michelle wondered.

Michael scooted his chair away from the table, "I'll go see."

"Hey Alex!" They heard him exclaim. "You are just in time for dinner."

"Sounds tempting but I really should get home to the girls. I came by to ask for a favor."

"Well come on in, at least let us make you a sandwich. Rose makes the best sloppy joes. You gotta try it!" said Michael bringing Alex into the kitchen.

"Hi Alex," smiled Michelle. "Have a seat."

"Thank you, I think I will," he said eyeing the sloppy joes hungrily.

"Rose made it special for me because I told her she looks purty, in her new dress," announced Jordan proudly, through a mouthful of food. "Don't you think she looks purty Alex?"

Alex looked at Rose. Yes, he definitely thought she looked pretty. He had in fact noticed it the moment he entered the kitchen but thought it better to refrain from mentioning it, but certainly now that someone brought it up there would be no harm done in agreeing. His green eyes twinkled mischievously. "Yes, Jordan, I think she looks very pretty," he smiled charmingly at Rose.

Rose busied herself with fixing Jaden's sandwich, wishing she could think of a witty reply, instead of blushing and feeling tongue-tied.

"These sloppy joes are great," Alex complimented. "You look like you're feeling better."

"Oh yes I feel much better."

"Well then I have a request. My grandmother that lives with me fell and broke her leg yesterday, so I am looking for someone who could come and stay with us for awhile and care for her and my two little girls. Does that sound like something you would be interested in doing?"

"If Michelle can spare me?" Rose looked questioningly at her employer.

"Yes I think we can work something out, if you can still come back and do the cleaning."

"Oh yes that would be fine," Alex agreed. "When can you start?"

"How about I bring her on Friday evening?" suggested Michelle.

"That would be great. I should be going, thanks for dinner. I'll see you Friday Rose."

"Are you sure it is with you ok if I go?" Rose asked Michelle after Alex left.

"Yes, I am getting around better all the time. If I need extra help, I will let you know."

"She knows how to cook, clean and sew, but we are going to have to help her with her banking and I'll have to help her shop for clothes" Michelle told Michael as they prepared for bed.

"I'll gladly leave that to you dear."

Michelle laughed. It felt good to laugh again. The past few months had been so traumatic trying to adjust to life with a missing leg.

"Michael, I uh was a wondering, does it bother you how I look now? I mean do you still find me attractive?" she blushed.

Michael leaned on his elbow looking at his wife lying beside him, his eyes dark with passion. "Let me put your mind at ease, my beautiful wife," he whispered pulling her into his embrace.

"Rose did your parents ever teach you how to do banking?" asked Michelle as they finished the breakfast dishes, the following morning.

"I learned it in school but I never had an opportunity to put it into practice."

"Well, then I will show you." Michelle said bringing her checkbook and taking a seat at the table.

Wiping her hands on the dishtowel, Rose came over to join her, eager to learn from her mentor.

"We were paying your father three hundred and fifty dollars a week to have you work-

"That's too much." Rose interrupted. "I am not worth that much."

"Oh yes you are. We have three checks to give you."

"But I didn't work the first week I was back."

"That's ok. Michael and I want you to have it, to help you get a good start. You will need it when the baby comes."

Rose did the math in her head, one thousand and fifty dollars. "I still think that is too much." she protested. "The most I have ever had before was twenty dollars in birthday money from my grandparents. I feel like a millionaire."

Michelle laughed. "It's a long way from a million dollars, but I remember how I felt when I started earning money. I also spent lots of it foolishly. I don't think you will do that, but I will do my best to help you avoid the mistakes I made."

“Thank you,” Rose said to the lady behind the counter who had helped her set up her bank account.

The lady nodded but didn’t respond.

Rose sighed with relief, grateful that the task was complete. Gathering up her papers, she turned to find Michelle.

“Is that really you Rose?” a familiar voice spoke behind her.

Roses’ heart sank; she hadn’t expected to meet anyone from the community here. Why oh why had she decided to leave the house with this dress and without a covering? She highly doubted she would feel worse if she were caught naked! Rose turned to greet her cousin Rebecca.

“Hi. What are you doing here?”

“I came to make a deposit for Dad,” Rebecca replied, her eyes quickly taking in every detail of Roses’ attire, denim jumper, white boots, and her long hair, unconfined by the usual bun and covering.

“Oh Rose!” Rebecca acted horrified, “Don’t you know what a sin you are committing by being dressed out of the *ordnung*? Your poor parents would weep if they saw you!”

“What I am wearing is modest,” Rose replied.

“Well whatever you do, do not cut your hair Rose,” Rebecca warned. “”Please just reconsider and come back! Your parents are heart broke at the way you up and left without telling anyone.”

Rose gasped disbelievingly. “It was not like that!” she protested.

Rebecca shook her head sadly. “There is also a rumor that you are pregnant by an outsider?”

“Maybe some other time and place would be better to have this discussion,” Michelle stepped up to Rebecca, interrupting her. Though the entire conversation had taken place in Pennsylvania Dutch and she hadn’t understood a word Rebecca had spoken to Rose, Michelle could clearly see the impact the conversation was having on Rose.

Rebecca, choosing to disregard Michelle's advice went on, "I do hope for your sake that the rumors are not true. If you so choose, you can come back right now, but with a child…" she paused for affect and clucked her tongue piously. "You certainly couldn't expect anyone to ever marry you!"

Every word felt like a dagger to her heart, Rose could only stare through teary eyes at the cousin she once shared such a loving relationship with. It was all too much.

"It's only because I love you that I have to do my duty and admonish you," Rebecca declared. Not waiting for a reply, Rebecca turned and walked away.

Taking a deep breath, Rose tried to compose herself. It would not do to make a further scene by bursting into tears.

"Shall we go?" asked Michelle laying a hand on her shoulder.

Rose nodded her head, not trusting herself to speak.

Once outside in the privacy of the Bennett's van, Rose's tears spilled over. "I can't believe she would act that way," she sobbed to Michelle who was listening sympathetically. "She said it was out of love that she admonished me. It did not feel like love!"

"You're right," Michelle agreed. "That is not love. Love builds us up, and it causes us to be kind and compassionate. I'm sorry she hurt you. Shall I pray for you?"

"Sure," Rose bowed her head feeling comforted by Michelle's prayer.

"Now are you ready to go shopping?" smiled Michelle.

"I can hardly wait," Rose smiled through her tears.

Chapter Fifteen

"I hope this room will be suitable." said Alex as he showed Rose to her room.

"Oh yes," answered Rose. "It is very nice," her eyes quickly taking in the huge walk-in closet, queen size log bed, and best of all her very own bathroom.

"The girls' bedroom is right next to yours," Alex pointed out. "I thought it would be good in case they wake up during the night, when I am not here. Sometimes I get called to the hospital during the night," he explained. "And my grandmother's room is just down the hall. She will want you to call her Mrs. Scott. She'll be home Monday."

"Oh Ok. Where are the girls?" asked Rose.

"My Aunt Cheryl had them for the night last night but they should be back shortly.

"I have never seen the inside of a log home before," Rose looked around at the huge fireplaces and the cathedral ceilings. "It is very beautiful, Alex."

"Thanks I love it. I inherited it from my grandfather. Caitlin loved it too," he shared.

"I am sure she did. Did she do the decorating?' asked Rose.

"Yes she did, she loved decorating."

"Is it ok to talk about Caitlin to the girls, or does it make them too sad?"

"They barely remember her," Alex said regretfully. "Lacy doesn't remember her at all. I tell them stories about her all the time though; I want them to remember her."

"I am sure that helps them feel like they have a Mommy that loves them."

"I suppose you are right," Alex agreed.

The front door burst open and both girls called out at once."Is she here Daddy?"

"Yes we are in the kitchen," he called.

"Sorry," he grinned apologetically. "They have yet to learn good manners."

Before Rose had time to respond, two little girls entered, smiling shyly.

"This is Taylor," introduced Alex, tousling her blond curls affectionately. She's four and this is my baby, Lacey."

"I'm not a baby!" interrupted Lacey. "I'm almost three," she said holding up three chubby little fingers to demonstrate. "Are you going to make my birthday cake?"

Rose smiled at the little girl. "Sure, what kind do you like?"

"I like chocolate," she replied coming to stand a bit closer.

"Chocolate is my favorite too," said Rose reaching out to take Lacey's hand.

Alex stood back and watched as his two daughters gravitated toward Rose, both of them talking at once. He grinned as he watched them take her by the hand and lead her away to their room to play Barbie.

"The girls absolutely adore you," said Alex one week later after he had finished tucking the girls in. Rose had been all they'd talked about.

"They are so sweet, I love them," said Rose as she took a pan of cookies from the oven.

"Even playing Barbie with them?" he teased.

"A girl never outgrows Barbie's, besides I never had one when I was little."

"Really?" Alex was surprised.

"Yes, the Amish ways are very strict, only homemade dolls without faces were allowed in our home."

"Why is that?" Alex asked curiously. He had always found the Amish very intriguing, and maybe that was his attraction to Rose, he told himself. Certainly it couldn't be anything else, he was very much in love with Caitlin still, and there could never be anyone else for him. Assuring himself of this, he settled down to enjoy Rose's company as he came to do every evening he was home.

"Amish believe that having a real doll would be too near like the graven images that the Bible speaks of." Rose explained.

"Do you believe that?" asked Alex pouring himself a cup of coffee and taking a hot cookie from the counter.

"Not anymore. I never gave it much thought before though, it was just another rule and no one is allowed to question the rules," she replied.

"Does anyone ever question the rules?" asked Alex.

"Not if they know what is good for them," laughed Rose.

The telephone rang preventing Alex's response. "Would you excuse me while I get that?"

"Sure go ahead."

Alex hurried to the phone. Picking it up, he was pleased to hear Michelle's voice on the other end of the line.

"Hey Alex, how's Rose working out?"

"Just great. Work is all that girl does."

"Thursday is her birthday. I was thinking of taking her to a salon to pamper her."

"That's nice. She deserves a break," said Alex.

"Do you think you could get someone to watch the girls that day?"

"Sure I'll check with Aunt Cheryl. Uhm, Michelle, how old will she be?"

"Twenty one. Why?" asked Michelle grinning into her phone.

"Just curious," said Alex.

"I have to go, the twins need me," Michelle said. Now remember don't tell her, I want it to be a surprise."

Hanging up the phone Alex made his way back to kitchen, disappointed that Rose had already retired for the evening.

"Michelle, what brings you here?" asked Rose welcoming her into the house.

"Happy birthday! I came to take you away for the day." She announced, loving the look of surprise on Rose's face.

"So, that is why Cheryl came to get the girls this morning."

"Yes, I okayed it with Alex the other night."

"What are we doing?"

"I'm taking you to a salon and spa."

"I, um, I do not know what that is?"

"That's ok," reassured Michelle. "It's a place where you get your hair done and all kinds of other good stuff. You'll see"

"Oh good, I have been thinking about getting my haircut."

"Do you feel free to do that?"

"Yes, I do now. All my life my parents told me that you can tell what is in a person's heart by the way they dress, but I found several verses that say that God does not judge according to the outward appearance, but He judges what is in our hearts."

"You are learning a lot," Michelle complimented. She loved Rose's openness and the way she always made sure it was ok with God's word before she accepted anything new.

"It feels so good to know I do not have to dress a certain way to be accepted, God loves me just the way I am." Rose declared happily.

"How shall I have it cut?" asked Rose nervously fingering her hair.

"What if you get it cut about here," said Michelle touching the middle of her back to demonstrate. "Then maybe just cut it around here to frame your face. I would have them cut a few layers in it, to make it lighter, your hair is so thick."

"I don't want to do anything to drastic," admitted Rose.

"Oh Rose, you just said don't," laughed Michelle. "I notice you never use contractions."

"*I'm* trying to change that," Rose grinned. "I guess I never realized until I came to your house how proper I spoke."

"Why do you talk so proper? Does everyone talk that way?"

"No, but a lot of people do. The reason I think I did was because I did not -didn't" she laughingly corrected herself. "I didn't learn how to speak English until I went to school and then I learned it just how you read it, very proper."

"Did you ever speak English at home?"

"No. Dad forbid it."

"Really? Why?"

"It was too much like the world." answered Rose.

"Are you ladies ready for your manicure?" asked a slim young girl in a white smock.

Rose looked questioningly at Michelle. "I promise you will like it," Michelle smiled.

Rose stuck her hands and feet out in front of her, admiring her shiny purple nails. "Oh Michelle, I feel like a queen even if I don't look like one."

"Why ever would you say that?" Michelle questioned.

"I guess I have always thought of myself as plain. I'm not pretty like Katie."

"You are very pretty. Didn't your mother ever tell you that?"

Rose shook her head. "No, no one ever tells anyone that they are pretty. It's considered prideful."

"Do you think it is prideful Rose?"

"I don't know," Rose shrugged.

"It is important to love yourself. The bible says love thy neighbor as thyself. If you don't love yourself, how can you love those close to you?"

"I never thought about it like that. But I will try and do that," promised Rose. "I want to do what is right."

"Thank you so much for today," Rose hugged Michelle before exiting the van. "I love my hair and this new dress. Thank you."

"My pleasure, I enjoyed it too" Michelle said.

"Oh Rose, you look so nice!" Taylor squealed delightedly.

"You have pretty purple nails," noticed Lacey.

Rose sat down in the recliner making room for both girls to climb up in her lap. She began to tell them all the things they had done at the salon.

"Yuck! Why did they put mud on your face?" Taylor wrinkled her nose in disgust.

"It's to help me look pretty," Rose explained, laughing at their reaction.

Alex watched the scene through the partially open office door. "Well, she certainly doesn't need any help looking pretty," he thought noticing her long hair and deep blue eyes.

"Can we take a picture of Rose?" asked Taylor bursting into his office several moments later.

"Sure, let me get the camera," said Alex joining them in the living room. "Do you mind Rose?"

"I have never had my picture taken before."

"Never? Why?"

Just then there was a knock at the door.

"Hang on a sec. I'll be right back," promised Alex heading toward the door. "I want to be the first person to take your picture."

Alex opened the door, his laughter ceasing. Who were all these people anyway?

"Is Rose here?" asked the leader, a tall man with a long gray beard and black broad brimmed hat.

Alex felt sick at the pit of his stomach. "This had to be Rose's father. He wanted to scream at him for the way he had beat Rose and for the scars that she still carried because of him. But it wasn't a choice he could make. It would be for Rose to decide. He clenched his jaws tightly to refrain from ordering Mr. Miller to leave his property.

Reaching behind him with his foot, he shut the door that lead to the living room. He had to give Rose some warning.

"Yes, she is here, she is taking care of the girls at the moment. Why don't you come in here," he ushered them into the dining room. Inviting them to have seats, he closed the door behind him and quickly made his way back to the living room.

"Taylor, Lacey, Daddy needs you to go to your room. I want to talk to Rose."

Both girls reluctantly slipped off Rose's lap and headed for their rooms.

"Is everything ok?" asked Rose.

"Your family is here to see you."

"Here?" she whispered her face turning ashen.

Alex nodded. "They are in the dining room. You don't have to see them if you don't want to."

"Is my father here too?" she asked fearfully.

Alex nodded. "I think so."

"What shall I do Alex? Shall I go change?" she panicked feeling like a child that had been caught disobeying.

"Do you feel like what you have on is wrong?" asked Alex.

"No, but they will think so."

"You are not doing anything wrong in God's eyes," Alex said gently.

"You are right," Rose agreed. "Please pray for me."

Alex reached out and caught her hand in his. "I am here if you need me." He watched her head toward the dining room feeling an overwhelming urge to run after her and protect her.

Rose breathed a quick prayer asking God to be with her and opened the door. She felt every eye on her as she entered the room. Forcing herself to look at her parents, she greeted them. Taking a quick look around the room, she noted that her entire family was present accompanied by Bishop Dan.

"We've come to take you home," Dad announced. "Go get your things," he ordered.

Rose felt her stomach tie in knots, at his command. "I can't do that," she said quietly. It was the first time she could remember refusing to obey his command.

"Can't or won't," he challenged.

Rose bit her lip, refusing to answer.

"You understand that if you don't come home with us, the next step we will take is to excommunicate you?" Bishop Dan asked. Several of her siblings burst into tears at his words.

"I have repented before God for my sins," Rose answered with a calm she did not feel. "He has forgiven me and I hope you will too."

"Not until you come back and confess before all the people," Dad said harshly.

One by one, her family pleaded with her to come back, some of them with tears and others with harsh words. Each one reminding her of the vow she had made at sixteen to remain with the Amish church until death.

"How can you disregard all the things your parents have taught you?" rebuked Bishop Dan.

"I haven't," Rose denied.

"I can see you are in rebellion by the way you are dressed." He argued.

"Oh Rose, please reconsider and come home." Mom pleaded.

Her tears were too much for Rose. "I am sorry Mom. I can't."

"You could if you really wanted to," Dad interjected. "If you were really sincere in your claim to be following Christ, you would pay me the money you owe me."

Rose looked shocked. "What money?"

"Remember you are not of age until you are twenty-one, therefore all the money you make and the money you've made the past several weeks belongs to me, as well as the clothes you were wearing the night you left. I paid for those too."

"I am sorry you feel that way, but I don't want to argue with you. I think it might be best if you left now." Rose said through her tears. "I love you all and I hope you can forgive me for anything I have done that offended or hurt you, it was not intended."

"Not intended!" Dad exploded, and for a second Rose feared he might hit her.

"You deliberately lied to us and like a harlot you slept with a man out of wedlock. Is this the man you slept with or was it yet another?" he asked implying that she was sleeping with Alex.

"That's enough!" Rose cried. "I want you to leave."

"You will never see any of your family again," he threatened. "We'll be forced to shun you. It is the last love we can show you according to scripture Rose." Putting his hat on he turned and left.

Rose turned and fled, unable to hold back her tears.

"Here come here," Alex reached out and grabbed her hand when she came through the kitchen.

"Oh Alex it was so horrible the things he said!" she cried.

Pulling her into his arms, Alex held her close. "It's going to be ok," he whispered.

"I am sorry Alex, I don't mean to be a crybaby."

"You have nothing to be sorry about," he reassured her. "Do you want to talk about it?"

Rose nodded.

"Here sit down and let me get you a cup of tea," Alex offered.

Alex listened as Rose told him of growing up with an unreasonably harsh father. And of her encounter with Lane, that had brought her into this mess.

"You haven't heard from him since?" he asked in amazement.

"No."

"Are you in love with him?" asked Alex.

"No, I just wanted to feel loved. He was the first person that ever told me I was beautiful. I can't believe I fell for it!" she berated herself.

"Don't be so hard on yourself. We all make mistakes."

"Enough about me. How did you meet Caitlin?" asked Rose ready to change the subject.

"We met in college. We were friends for a while before we began dating."

"I think that is the best." said Rose.

A comfortable silence settled between the two, both of them reluctant to go their separate ways.

Chapter Sixteen

"Are you comfortable, Mrs. Scott?" asked Rose carefully adjusting her pillows.

"I guess as well as I can be in these circumstances," she grumbled.

"If there's anything else you need let me know." Rose said before closing the door.

"I know what I'd like to get her," muttered Rose as she headed back to the kitchen.

"And just what would that be," Alex whispered behind her.

Rose jumped startled. "What are you doing home Alex?" Color rushed to her cheeks.

"I think it's time for you to take a break," Alex chuckled.

"I could take the girls to the park while you watch her."

"That is not a break," Alex said. "Come with me," he said leading the way into the living room.

"I'm sorry about what I said," Rose began.

"It's ok, believe me. I know she can be very difficult and you have been taking care of her around the clock. You need a break," he insisted. Why don't you go to the mall or something?"

"I can't drive," answered Rose. "And I don't really have any place to go."

"That's ok. I can teach you," offered Alex.
"You wouldn't mind?"
"Not at all." In fact, he could hardly wait.

"How are you doing Rose?" asked Michelle as the two of them sat down to begin their weekly bible study and mentoring class. She was currently mentoring two other women, but she realized, as she prepared her notes, she enjoyed her time with Rose the most.

"I don't feel like I'm doing very well," Rose admitted. "I had a rough week. I burned a hole in Alex's shirt when I was ironing, and then Taylor gave Lacey a haircut when I was bathing Mrs. Scott. I think Alex is sorry he hired me."

"I don't think so. You have to concentrate on the one hundred things you did right not on the two or three things that you did wrong. Satan will try and get you to focus on your shortcomings, what you need to do, is rejoice in all the things you do right." Michelle encouraged.

"I never thought about it like that. I do need you to pray for me about being able to forgive my father." Rose requested. "I have tried to forgive him but I just feel so angry at him still!"

"We will take a look at what the bible says about forgiveness today," Michelle decided. "But remember that forgiveness is a choice, not a feeling. You won't have a fuzzy warm feeling as soon as you make the choice to forgive him. Every time you think about how he hurt you, say to yourself, I choose to forgive, and then put it from your mind and focus on God and other positive things in your life. Forgiveness is something we sometimes need to do more than once."

"Are you sure that you are ready for this?" asked Alex as he opened the driver's side door.

"I am nervous. I'm afraid that I might wreck your car." Rose answered.

"You'll be fine, just follow my instructions."

"I'll try."

"Here is the brake and this is the clutch," Alex explained how to work each component.

"I hope I can remember everything you said." Rose sighed. "It sounds very complicated."

"You'll do fine. Put your left foot on the clutch and your right foot on the brake and turn the key."

Rose followed each instruction carefully.

"Now take your right foot off the brake and slowly let up on the clutch."

Rose complied, but grimaced when the jeep lurched forward and the engine died.

She was ready to quit after several more failed attempts and told her instructor as much.

"I'll guide you through it," Alex laughed placing his hand over hers on the stick shift.

Rose tensed at his touch, butterflies dancing in her stomach.

"Is everything ok?" asked Alex noticing her uneasiness.

"I, um, its just that you make me nervous," she snapped.

Alex chuckled, keeping his hand firmly over hers. "That can be a good thing," he said holding her gaze with his own.

Rose blushed and quickly dropped her eyes to the steering wheel, deciding to ignore his remark and try again, but once again she missed her cue letting out the clutch too fast on the third gear and stalling out the motor.

Rose hung her head. "I can't do it right."

"You can do it, Rose. It's ok not to do everything perfect all the time. Just relax."

"What does that mean? I'm not trying to be perfect," she flared. "I'm just trying to do it right."

"You are always trying to be perfect. You think you can never allow yourself to make a mistake." Alex argued.

"That is not true!" Rose denied. "I think that is horrible for you to say that!"

"Rose," Alex tried a gentler approach. "No matter how hard you try to do everything perfect, you cannot make up for the mistakes you made in the past."

Not giving him time to finish Rose opened her door to get out. "I am not going to talk about it."

"Why?" Alex challenged. "Because it's true?"

"No it's not true," Rose turned her back and began walking away.

"Rose please come back," Alex pleaded.

Ignoring his plea, Rose continued walking. Who did he think he was? And why did men think they always had to boss her anyway?

Rose walked on toward the park, anger at Alex and his words boiling inside her.

It's the truth that hurts, the old adage popped into her mind. Certainly that was not the case here, Rose decided turning back toward home ignoring her conscience. There was absolutely nothing wrong with trying to do ones best.

Still angry with Alex and not yet ready to consult her Savior, Rose marched into the house, hoping Alex had been called away to the hospital.

Checking on Mrs. Scott and making sure she was ok, Rose headed toward the kitchen. Might as well unload the dishwasher, she decided hoping the chore would help her calm down a bit. Spotting some toys on the floor that Lacey had left lying earlier, Rose bent down to retrieve them.

Whack! Rose bit her lip from crying out. Someone had left the cupboard door open and she had stood up under it. Tears stung her eyes as she rubbed her head.

"Are you ok?" asked Alex choosing that very moment to enter the kitchen.

Rose nodded, keeping her back turned.

Coming over to stand in front of her, Alex reached out and touched her chin turning her head. "Let me have a look," he said gently.

"I'll be ok," she said tearfully.

"I'm sorry about earlier," Alex tipped her head back, forcing her eyes to meet his. "You didn't let me finish Rose."

When Rose did not answer, he continued. "We can never be good enough on our own, and no amount of good works will make up for our past mistakes. We must trust in Jesus for that."

"I'm sorry, I didn't give you a chance to explain." Rose apologized. She could hardly think of anything else at the moment but the weak feeling in her knees.

"I'm sorry too," he said huskily dropping his hand onto her shoulder his eyes never leaving hers. Slowly he moved his hand up the side of her neck feeling her pulse against the palm of his hand.

Rose felt her heartbeat accelerate at his gentle touch. Looking into his deep green eyes, Rose knew she wanted to receive his kiss as much as he wanted to give it.

Ring. The untimely ringing of the telephone broke the spell and the two stepped apart, Alex turning quickly to answer it. Rose leaned against the counter behind her for support, taking a deep breath.

"I'll be right there," Rose heard him say, feeling a mixture of regret and relief.

"Hospital called," Alex called over his shoulder. "It might be late before I get back."

Rose emptied the dishwasher, and bathed the girls, her mind replaying the scene between her and Alex. Her Dad's harsh words *like a harlot* … Oh surely she wasn't that. Tucking the girls in, Rose looked at the clock it was eight forty-five, maybe she could call Michelle and talk things over.

"Oh Michelle, what is wrong with me? I *wanted* Alex to kiss me!"

Michelle laughed. "That is a perfectly normal emotion Rose. Feeling that way does not make you a sinner. The important thing is that you make a commitment to God to keep yourself pure and not act on your emotions."

"No one ever talked to me about sex and purity before," said Rose.

"So before you were with Lane you didn't know anything about it at all?" asked Michelle sounding shocked. "Didn't your mother explain certain things?"

"No my mother never told me anything about sex. When I began my menstrual cycle, I had to ask her what was happening. She supplied me with the necessary items and explained that it was part of a woman's curse because of Eve's sin," Rose recounted the experience.

"How come no one talks about it?" asked Michelle.

"I think it's because everyone is so private. I remember as a little girl we would talk with our little girlfriends about holding hands and kissing our boyfriends when we grew up, but there was never any mention of sex even by the older people."

"So how did it happen that you slept with Lane?"

"I had a crush on Lane for years, and that night he talked so sweet to me, and told me how beautiful and special I was. No one had ever told me that before. I wanted so much to feel loved. When the time came, I should've said no, I felt like I would be disappointing him, and then he wouldn't think I was special or beautiful anymore," finished Rose.

"Do you love Lane?"

"No, I just had a crush on him but believe me he cured me of that," she said remembering painfully his harsh words the following morning.

"You do realize that someday he will have to know about the baby right?"

"I hoped I would never have to face him again. How will I tell him?"

"Can you call him or write to him?" asked Michelle.

"No. I don't have any way to contact him."

"I'll try and help you figure it out, and I will teach you what the Bible says about purity."

Chapter Seventeen

"Today is Valentine's day. Would you like to help me make some cookies?"

"Yes, yes," said both girls excitedly.

"Can we decorate them with pink and red frosting?" asked Taylor.

"Yes, and you can put sprinkles on them too," said Rose getting out several bowls and the ingredients needed to get started. "My Mom used to let me make cookies for Valentine's Day too." The memories of her and Katie competing to make the best dessert made her homesick.

"Can I stir something?" begged Lacey climbing up on the table.

"In a minute you can stir the butter and sugar," said Rose, "but you may not sit on the table."

And that was just the beginning. Taylor knocked the eggs off the table, and Lacey dumped the canister of sugar on the floor.

Trying to remain calm, Rose put Lacey in her high chair and Taylor in a booster seat telling them to stay put until the dough was ready to cut out.

The dough was soon finished and Rose supplied the girls with cookie cutters, showing them how to roll out the dough.

"Rose," Grandma Scott chose that precise moment to call her away from her task.

"Stay in your seats until I come back," Rose instructed hurrying toward the Mrs. Scott's room.

Mrs. Scott was in a particularly cantankerous mood that morning, wanting everything just a certain way. "Could you turn my television screen a bit? And I would like you to adjust those shades so the plants get more sunlight." The list went on. Rose looked anxiously at her watch; she had been away from the girls for ten minutes already. Remembering the mess they had created while she'd been with them she feared what they were up to in her absence.

A loud cry coming from the kitchen, confirmed her fears.

"Oh no I had better go check on the girls," exclaimed Rose leaving a very disgruntled Mrs. Scott in the bathroom.

Reaching the kitchen, Rose spotted Lacey standing on a chair in front of the drawer where the sharp knives were kept, blood running down her arm. Quickly grabbing a paper towel Rose wrapped it around her hand.

"There now it's going to be ok." Rose soothed, trying to quiet her.

"I'm sorry," Taylor cried. "I told her she couldn't have it. I tried to take it away," she confessed.

Rose slowly pulled back the towel, cringing when she saw the cut. It would definitely require stitches, she decided, wrapping it up again. "Shall we put an ice pack on it?"

Lacey nodded, calming down a bit.

"I will call Daddy and he will take care of you," Rose comforted hugging her close.

Rose groaned inwardly, that meant she would have to call Alex. She hadn't really spoken to him in over a week, not since the incident in the kitchen. He had been putting in long hours at the hospital, and the two of them had only talked in passing.

Locating the number on the fridge, Rose picked up the phone and dialed Alex's office.

"Dr. Scott's office." answered the receptionist.

"Yes this is Rose, Is Alex there?"

"He is with a patient. Could I take a message?"

"Yes please," Rose answered relaying her message.

"Let me put you on hold and I'll go see if I can get him the message," offered the receptionist.

She was back several moments later. "He will be home in a few minutes."

"Thanks," Rose hung up the phone.

"Oh no, I have to go help your Grandma," she told the girls remembering that she left the poor lady in the bathroom.

Taking the girls in the den and putting them on the couch she instructed Taylor to turn on the television, while she aided Mrs. Scott, hoping the television program would distract Lacey for a few minutes.

"I'm sorry," Rose apologized as she entered the bathroom. "I was making cookies with the girls and Lacey cut herself."

"She really shouldn't have been left alone where she could get a knife," rebuked the elderly lady.

"You're right," said Rose, wanting to remind Mrs. Scott that she couldn't be two places at once.

"Children shouldn't be allowed to help with adult chores," she said. "It's too dangerous. You have to be more organized."

Rose didn't respond. She just wanted to go hold Lacey. Her heart sank when she heard Alex come through the front door. Now the girls were alone again! Helping Mrs. Scott back into her bed, she quickly went in search of Alex.

"Oh Lord please help me get through this," she prayed as she made her way to the den.

"Where are the girls?" asked Alex anxiously.

"I put them in the den, while I went to help Mrs. Scott," she explained.

"Try not to leave them alone," Alex reprimanded her heading for the den.

Taking a quick look at Lacey's hand, Alex pronounced the need for a few stitches, and picking her up, he headed for the door. "I'm taking her in to my office," he said over his shoulder. "I'll take Taylor too," and without another word he was gone.

Rose headed for the kitchen. "What a disaster area." Taylor had dumped the entire bottle of red food coloring into the icing, and Lacey had dropped her cookie dough on the floor.

"No wonder Alex took Taylor with him," she sighed dismally. "He is probably scared to leave them alone with me now. Maybe he thinks I am nothing but a dumb Amish girl too." A tear slid down her cheek and then another. Self pity set in and soon the tears began to flow faster.

Heading for the broom closet, Rose got out the cleaning supplies and began with the kitchen. "Maybe cleaning will make me feel better," she thought miserably as she scrubbed at the red food coloring that had spilled.

"Maybe I would be better off at home. I wouldn't have to worry about where I am going to live and how I am going to support myself after I get done here. Who is going to take care of me when the baby is born? At home, Mom would take care of me." Rose swept up the sugar.

"Dear Lord Jesus, please help me know what to do." she prayed. "Yes, going home would be easier," she said to herself remembering fondly all the cousins, aunts and uncles. There would family at Christmas and other special occasions. But who will I have now if I stay?"

"I will never leave thee nor forsake thee," The words of Jesus whispered comfort to her heart.

Rose felt a peace filling her heart. "Jesus you are all I need."

Humming happily, Rose finished the cleaning. "It's not too late to make it a happy day," she decided. "I will make Lacey's favorite dessert and spaghetti for the main course," she decided.

Standing back to survey her work, Rose felt pleased with her accomplishments. The kitchen was clean and dinner was ready. She could hardly wait for Alex and the girls to come home. "Where are they anyway?" she looked at her watch. It was 5:00.

"Well, it's time for Mrs. Scott to eat," she took special pains preparing her an attractive looking tray. "Maybe this will cheer her up," she said heading toward the bedroom.

Just then the front door was flung open and both girls came bursting in all smiles. "Look, look, we got a puppy!"

"That's nice," smiled Rose dropping down on one knee and greeting the new addition. "What is the puppy's name?"

"We named her Pepper," Lacey informed her. "Daddy said that is a good name for a girl puppy."

"I used to have a puppy named Seven." Rose said.

"Can the puppy sleep in our room Daddy?" the girls begged.

"We'll see," promised Alex.

"We'll go show her our room right now," Taylor announced running toward the stairs with Lacey and Pepper tight on her heels.

"I would like to talk tonight after the girls go to bed if that's ok with you?" Alex looked at Rose.

"Yes." Rose answered. "I have to go reheat your Grandma's supper," she excused herself.

Alex watched her as she walked away. He knew he needed to talk to her but what was he going to say. He had struggled with it all week. Caitlin was gone forever. But, at twenty- eight I may have another forty or fifty years. The thought of living all those years without someone to share it with, was overwhelmingly lonely.

"Does that mean I'm ready to start dating?" he asked himself. "Definitely not," he decided. "So then what am I going to say to Rose?" he shook his head helplessly.

Running the bathwater for the girls, Rose headed to the living room to find Pepper and put her outside. Not seeing Taylor's backpack lying on the floor, Rose tripped pitching headlong toward the floor.

"Watch out!" Alex who had also come in search of Pepper too reached out to grab her arm.

"Thanks," Rose breathed a sigh of relief. "I'm getting so clumsy.

"Are you ok?" Alex asked.

"Yes, I just tripped over this backpack."

"I, I just wanted to say I am sorry about what happened last week."

"That's ok," Rose said. "I am the one who should apologize."

"No, I mean, about well, about what almost happened." Alex finished nervously.

"I know I wanted you to kiss me too," she confessed.

Alex felt his heart melt at her innocent confession. He also felt relieved that it wasn't one sided.

"I like you a lot, but I am not ready for, I mean, uh, not that, that you are asking," Rose blushed miserably. "I want us to be friends, if that is what you want."

Alex reached out and squeezed her hand. "I would love us to be friends."

"Can we watch a movie tonight Daddy?" Lacey begged of Alex several days later after dinner was over.

"Shouldn't you be in bed already?" Alex teased.

"Please?" Taylor begged. "Can we ask Rose to watch it with us?"

"I'll go ask her," offered Alex, he had noticed that Rose never watched T.V. so he wasn't sure if she would want to or not.

"Would you like to watch a movie with us?" asked Alex finding Rose in the kitchen.

"I don't know," Rose said hesitantly. "I never watched a movie."

"Why? Do think it's wrong?" Alex asked knowing how conscientious she was.

"I guess I was always taught that it was wrong. What do you think?"

"I think if you watch something that is morally clean, it's no different than reading a good book."

"I think that it would be ok then," she agreed. "I'll watch it."

"I'll make the popcorn," Alex offered, "and you go tell the girls."

Rose laughed at the girls' reaction. They immediately insisted that she join them on the recliner.

"Are you sure there is room for me?"

"Yes," they insisted. "Daddy always sits with us."

Alex soon appeared with the popcorn and everyone settled down to watch the movie.

Rose sat spellbound as the story unfolded before her. "I like this," she smiled at Alex. "This is so much fun! Did you have a T.V. when you were growing up too?"

"Yes, but my parents were very strict and we weren't allowed to watch much T.V."

Rose didn't comment she was lost in the story again.

Alex grinned; he enjoyed watching Roses' amazement over the movie. His heart warmed at the picture of his two daughters cuddled up with Rose. For a moment, he felt a pang of regret that it wasn't Caitlin in Rose's place. Determined to enjoy the evening, Alex turned his attention back to the screen.

The movie was over and both the girls and Rose had fallen asleep. Alex took Lacey and then Taylor and put them to bed.

"Rose," Alex said quietly. "The movie is over." Bending down till his face was inches away he touched her arm. "Rose, time for bed."

"Um," she sighed. Reaching up she touched his face and pulled it close to her own and kissed him tenderly on the lips.

Alex felt his heart pounding in his chest, wanting with everything in him to return her kiss. "But how could he?" he groaned. She was fast asleep!

"Night, night," she murmured snuggling down further into the recliner.

Finding a blanket he covered her up. She could sleep here. Unable to resist, he brushed back her hair and kissed her cheek.

"I better get to bed," he decided, "before this whole friendship thing goes out the window."

Chapter Eighteen

Rose rubbed her hands nervously on her skirt. She had practically memorized the instruction manual, but she still felt like a little girl back in school, unprepared for a big test.

"It was Tuesday afternoon and Alex had dropped Rose off at the DMV office to get her drivers permit. She had studied all weekend, but she had still felt stumped by several of the questions. "Oh Lord, please help me get it right," she prayed as she made her way to the front counter. The lady at the counter had been rude, abrupt and anything but helpful when she first came in, leading Rose to believe that the lady might possibly count them all wrong just for the pleasure of making her life miserable.

Approaching the desk, Rose handed in her paper and held her breath as the lady checked it over.

"You have three wrong," the lady looked at Rose. "But you still passed so fill out this paper."

Rose tried hard to follow her instructions very carefully, her hands trembling with excitement.

"I did it!" Rose gushed happily on the phone to Michelle. "I was so scared! By the way the lady stared at me I thought for sure she must know everything about me. I thought she probably knows I am ex-Amish girl with only an eighth grade education. She made feel like I was doing something wrong, like I was cheating or something! Do people ever make you feel that way?"

"Yes, sometimes," answered Michelle trying to hold back her laughter at Rose's description. She loved the way she always said exactly what was on her mind.

"Do you still feel like people look at you funny Rose?"

"Yes, even when I have other clothes on, I still feel like I'm different, like I just don't fit in anywhere. I know I couldn't fit in if I went back, but I don't feel like I fit in here either. It's hard."

"That'll change with time," Michelle encouraged. "Everything is still so new. I think once you make more friends it'll be different."

"I suppose you're right. I will just have to be patient," agreed Rose.

"Why don't I pick you up Friday night and we'll go see a movie?" asked Michelle.

"I would like that, if Alex can get someone else to help out."

"I'm sure that won't be a problem," Michelle assured. "Aunt Cheryl is always happy to help out."

"Are you ready to try out that new permit?" asked Alex after dinner was over.

"Yes but I am nervous," admitted Rose, remembering how badly things went the last time.

"Cheryl will and stay with Grandma and the girls while we're gone," Alex informed her.

"We'll go out on a quiet country road," Alex informed her taking the wheel. "This time you can drive an automatic. That will be easier, and there won't be any other traffic to worry about."

"That's good. I don't think that I could handle driving in traffic."

They soon reached their destination and Rose slid behind the wheel. Riding Abby was so much easier, she thought wishing she could back out.

"Just relax," Alex advised. "This will be much easier than driving the stick."

"Put your foot on the brake and put the car in drive," Alex instructed.

Rose followed the instructions, anxious to get it just right.

"Now let up on the brake"-

Taking her foot off the brake, Rose panicked when the car began to roll forward and quickly returned her foot to the brake, nearly throwing Alex through the windshield.

"Easy on the brake," Alex grinned.

"I think I am getting the hang of this," said Rose a little while later, feeling a bit more confident.

"You're doing great," Alex encouraged.

"Oh no!" Rose panicked spotting a bunny hopping across the field and toward the road.

"I'll beat him," Rose quickly decided pressing a bit harder on the accelerator. But having under estimated the speed of the little animal, he hopped out into the road in front of her. Having a sudden change of heart, he turned to go back. Seeing the bunny in the center of the road Rose swerved hard to the right to miss the little critter, only to discover she had run off the road and still managed to hit him.

"Oh no," Rose groaned upon hearing the little ker-thunk. She quickly applied the brake and put the car in park. "I hit it, didn't I?"

Alex glanced in the review mirror and nodded, wondering how Rose being a former farm girl, would react to this tragedy.

"I have to make sure it's dead," said Rose reluctantly getting out of the vehicle.

"Oh no," she cried upon seeing the poor bunny lying helpless beside the road. "I injured it beyond repair. Do you have a hammer or something in the car to finish it off? I can't leave it suffering like this."

Alex left to check the trunk, thankful that Rose hadn't started crying.

"Sorry, I don't have anything," he came back empty handed. "I've never killed an animal," he admitted.

"There is only one thing left to do," Rose said resolutely.

"What's that?" Alex asked curiously.

"Hit it again," she replied very matter of fact, heading back toward the car.

The humor of the situation was too much. Alex dissolved in a fit of laughter. "Who else but Rose could be so practical?"

"We'll stop at the church first," Michelle informed Rose after picking her up on Friday evening.

"Shall I wait in the car for you?" asked Rose as they drove into the church parking lot.

"I'd like you to come in and help me get some books from the church library," requested Michelle.

"Looks like quite a few others are here tonight too," commented Rose, noticing several other cars in the parking lot.

"Maybe they are having a meeting," Michelle said, trying to keep from giggling. Poor Rose didn't suspect a thing! Inside the ladies were waiting to throw her a surprise baby shower. It had all been planned two weeks ago, and it had been up to Michelle to find a way to get Rose to the church.

"Surprise!" everyone called out as Rose opened the door to the fellowship hall.

"What?" Rose asked, looking confused.

"It's your baby shower," smiled Michelle.

"You tricked me!"

"I hope that's ok?" she teased.

Rose smiled and hugged her friend. "Thank you, but I really don't feel worthy of all this," she said looking around the room. There were pink, blue, yellow and green balloons. A beautiful cake was set up on a table with lots of snack foods. Nearly all the ladies from the church were present, many of whom she barely knew. She suddenly felt like crying, God saw how much she missed her family and He was giving her a new one.

"I just can't believe you did all this for me," Rose said over and over as she enjoyed her evening. She'd received gifts not just for the coming baby, but for herself as well.

"Look at all this stuff!" said Rose as she loaded everything into the back of Michelle's van. "I got a high chair, a crib, clothes, a car seat, and that is just to name a few," she said excitedly. "I can't believe all these people who barely know me would do this for me."

"That is our way of showing you God's love," Michelle said. "I'm glad you enjoyed it."

"It has made me realize that very soon I'm actually going to have a baby. I have been scared, worried and ashamed about it all, but tonight, well, it meant so much to see that no one was judging me and everyone is excited about the baby."

Rose placed her hands on her stomach. "I have regretted not having a special someone that was looking forward to the coming of this baby with me, and the thought of having no family was hard. But, after tonight, I feel like I do have a family." Rose said gratefully.

"I'm here for you if you ever need anything." Michelle offered.

"Well, I've been meaning to ask if I could stay with you for a week or so after I have the baby."

"Yes, I would love that! Are you hoping for a boy or girl?"

"I don't care, although I think a girl would be nice."

"How much longer until you are done at Alex's house?"

"We haven't talked about it, but I think Mrs. Scott is getting stronger every day. She will probably be up and around in another couple weeks."

"What will you do then?"

"Sharon Wilmer from church offered me her basement apartment. She needs someone to help care for her elderly mother that is coming to stay with her for the summer. I want to pray about it, but that would be a perfect solution for me."

Chapter Nineteen

"It feels like the greatest accomplishment of my life." declared Rose.

"I remember feeling that way too when I got my driver's license," Michelle agreed. "Now I look back and realize how immature I was to have such a huge responsibility."

"How did the test go?" asked Michael. "I barely passed mine."

Rose groaned. "I was so nervous. I prayed before I got there that the grouchy lady would not be my instructor. But, my prayer didn't get answered because the grouchy lady was the one who took me on the road test. She looked very stern and she kept writing things on her clip board. When I asked her how I was doing she didn't answer. By the time we got back I was so scared I hadn't passed. I was certainly glad she didn't know the bunny story though I felt like she did," added Rose.

"You are too funny," Alex laughed.

Rose laughed too. "Thank you for coming." The Bennett's, Alex and the girls were celebrating her success by going out for pizza. "At home everything was so tense and serious. I remember when I was little and us kids would start laughing, my mom would say: Don't laugh too much. Don't you know that you are going to cry as much as you laugh someday?"

"Really," Michelle was amazed; she loved to hear her children laugh and have fun. "I know it's not good to be silly all the time, but the bible says '*a merry heart doeth good like a medicine.* '"

"Amish people, or at least many of them are very superstitious."

"What do they believe?" asked Alex curiously.

"Some of them believe that if you stick a knife above your door, and sleep with your Bible under your pillow, it will keep out the evil spirits." Becoming aware that she was the center of attention, Rose apologized. "I'm sorry to be talking so much."

"That's ok; you were just answering our questions." Michelle reassured.

"And we enjoyed your answers," Alex grinned getting to his feet. "I really hate to be the one to break up this lovely party but I have an early morning, so I had better go."

"Thanks again," Rose said appreciatively. "You all make me feel like family."

"I would like to wring his little neck." muttered Rose as she cleaned up the puppy's third mess of the day. "He is impossible to train." Hearing the phone ring; Rose hurriedly put the cleaning supplies away before answering it.

"Hello," she spoke into the receiver.

"Who is this?" demanded an impatient female voice on the other end of the line. "I want to speak to Mrs. Scott."

"Mrs. Scott can't come to the phone." answered Rose wondering who the rude caller was.

"Who are you?" the lady demanded.

"I am the Scott's housekeeper." answered Rose a bit hesitantly not sure how much information she wanted to give the unknown caller.

"Well in that case tell Alex that his in-laws are coming back from Florida and we will be spending the weekend at his house. And by the way," she announced, "I am Mrs. Cole."

"I'll tell Alex you called."

"Since when has Alex had a housekeeper?" Demanded Mrs. Cole.

"I came in January after Mrs. Scott broke her leg."

"I see. Well he never bothered to hire a housekeeper for poor Caitlin. My other line is ringing. I've got to get that." Then hung up without a goodbye.

Rose hung up the phone, "I think I'll just leave when they get here." She looked at the calendar. "They'll be here in two days," she headed back to the broom closet, knowing the house would have to be spotless for this particular caller.

Rose breathed a sigh of relief; the cleaning was done, and the Cole's were expected to arrive shortly. All there was left to do was bathe the girls and get dinner.

Starting the water for the girls to take their bath, Rose hurried to make one more round through the house with the feather duster, making sure everything was clean.

"May I wear my new dress?" asked Lacey throwing her wet towel on the bedroom floor.

"How about this one instead?" asked Rose holding up a cute little denim dress.

"I don't like that one!" pouted Lacey. "I want my new one."

"The new one is to wear for church and special occasions," Rose explained patiently.

"But I want the new one!" cried Lacey.

About to go to battle with the youngster, Rose opened her mouth to explain that it was out of the question when the pealing of the doorbell interrupted.

"Ok put it on," Rose handed her the dress, hating to give in, but knowing now was not the time to engage in conflict. "Hurry and get dressed. Grandma is here."

She hurried down the stairs to answer the door, wishing Alex was home.

Putting on a polite smile, she opened the door.

"Where is everyone?" demanded Mrs. Cole looking past her.

"The girls are getting dressed, and Alex isn't home from work yet."

"I would've thought he'd have made the effort to be here. Wait, you didn't tell me you were pregnant." her tone was accusing. "How much longer till the baby comes?"

"About a month," answered Rose, wishing she wouldn't have to answer. The arrival of Taylor and Lacey prevented any further questions, and Rose quickly slipped away to the kitchen.

"It's as if Caitlin were never here, Alex!" Mrs. Cole scolded. "Where is that teapot collection I gave her, or those cute ceramic kittens she collected?"

"I had those packed up and put away for the girls, Arlene. It was too much for my grandmother to take care of." Alex said firmly.

Mrs. Cole opened her mouth to respond but Alex held up his hand. "Why don't we enjoy the evening and after the girls go to bed we can discuss it."

"Way to go Alex," Rose cheered under her breath removing the chicken from the oven.

Putting the finishing touches on the dinner, Rose headed for the living room.

"Dinner is on the table, Alex," she announced. "I'll have mine with Mrs. Scott."

"What do you mean, she lives here?" Rose heard Mrs. Cole demand as she carried her tray into Mrs. Scott's bedroom. In less than an hour the cantankerous old Mrs. Scott had become a saint that Rose looked forward to sharing her dinner with.

"Only one more day of this," Rose consoled herself as she entered her bedroom. It was Saturday afternoon and she had been relieved of most of her duties the past two days. Mrs. Cole had insisted in taking over the entire house.

"I'll work on my baby afghan," Rose said to herself. Opening the closet door, she pulled the partly finished afghan off the top shelf, only to have something land on her head.

"Ouch!" Rose cried rubbing her head. "What is this?" she picked up the black garment and inspected it. "This is my old coat from home. I forgot I even put it there."

Reaching into the pocket she pulled out a candy bar. "That's where it went." She smiled as she remembered the elderly couple that helped her. Reaching into the pocket again, she pulled out a handkerchief and a small white card.

Flipping over the card she gasped. "Mr. Charles Nelson! Was it possible that they were Kristen's grandparents?"

Rose sat on the bed trying to collect her thoughts. "Had they told Kristen they'd seen her? No that wasn't possible, they didn't know who she was. She shuddered as she thought of the horrible fear and pain she'd suffered that night. "Thank you God for taking care of me and for helping me come so far since then."

"There's only one thing to do," she decided, that was to call and thank the Nelsons and see if they really were Kristen's grandparents. Maybe they could put her in touch with Kristen. She could tell Kristen about the baby first and then it might not be so hard to tell Lane.

Making her way down the stairs to go use the phone, Rose rehearsed what she would say to the kind old couple. Hi I'm the girl you helped, or maybe she should start by asking if they were Kristen's grandparents.

Wanting some privacy to make her call, Rose slipped into Alex's office and closed the door. She looked curiously around the room. Alex had never asked her to clean in here and since the door was always closed she had never ventured inside.

It was definitely a man's room. Certificates and awards lined one entire wall while another wall was decorated with black silhouettes of horses and other western paraphernalia. Rustic log furniture, and a big leather chair completed the look.

"It smells good in here," said Rose, noticing the hint of Alex's cologne in the air. "But it needs to be cleaned," she brushed the dust off the corner of the desk.

Looking at the card, she dialed the Nelson's number. Rose waited anxiously.

"Hello," came the soft voice of an elderly lady.

"Hi, um, I don't know if you remember me or not but I am the girl you helped, you gave me some candy bars," Rose ran out of breath her words tumbling over each other.

"Yes! Yes! I remember," exclaimed the sweet old lady. "Are you ok? We have thought about you so often!"

"Yes," I'm fine."

"Oh that is good. Is there anything you need?"

"Well I was wondering if you have a granddaughter named Kristen?"

"Yes we certainly do. She's away at college. You must be her friend. Oh Kristen was so worried it was you when we told her about you. Of course we didn't know it was you, and neither did Kristen. She was so worried," repeated Mrs. Nelson.

"Could you please give Kristen my number and tell her I called?" requested Rose.

"Why yes dear. Just let me get a pen and paper.

"Thank you so much," Rose said giving her Alex's home phone number.

Rose smiled happily as she put the phone back on the hook. Closing the door behind her, she headed back toward the stairs, stopping when she heard Mrs. Cole say her name. Knowing she shouldn't eavesdrop, but unable to resist the temptation she crept a little closer.

"Well I don't care what you say," she told her husband. "It's not proper that Rose is living here. What do other people think? Look at her, pregnant out of wedlock. She obviously has no morals. Besides," she continued her rant. "I'm sure Alex is too nice to tell her to get out.

Rose had heard more than enough. Retreating, she fled to her room.

Chapter Twenty

"Who did she think she was anyway?" Rose fumed angrily. She'd been pacing in her room for nearly an hour, reliving every unkind word.

Grabbing her afghan she began knitting, her needles clicking furiously. "What made Mrs. Cole so unkind anyway?" She looked out the window at the rainy dreary weather. "It looks outside, like I feel on the inside," thought Rose dismally.

"Do people really think badly of Alex because of me? The last thing I want to do is ruin his reputation. I will talk to him about it the first chance I get," she decided.

Three days went by and Rose still hadn't gotten an opportunity to approach Alex. It was Tuesday evening, and she had just finished helping Mrs. Scott retire for the evening. Gathering her courage, she went in search of Alex. Unable to locate him in the living room, Rose headed toward his office. Hearing his voice inside Rose hesitated; maybe she should knock or even come back later.

"Believe me I wish she wouldn't be here either," came Alex's voice. I want to get rid of her but I can't. The girls absolutely adore her."

Choking back a sob, Rose ran to her room.

"Hang on Jake, I think I heard something," Alex opened his door and looked down the hall. "I don't see anything; it was probably that wretched little puppy. Like I was saying I'd like to get rid of the good for nothing varmint, but the girls love her, so that is out of the question!"

Rose reached over and shut off her alarm. It had been a long night of tossing and turning. Her head ached from crying and lack of sleep. "Maybe a long shower will help," she said crawling out of bed. The girls wouldn't be up for another hour, giving her plenty of time.

Finished with her shower, Rose got dressed and headed down stairs to get a cup of coffee. "I'll call Michelle," she headed for the phone. "She always helps me make sense of things."

Reaching for the phone, Rose stopped when she heard a soft knock at the door. "Who could be here this early?" she wondered heading for the door.

"It can't be!" Rose exclaimed in Pennsylvania Dutch. "Lena!" she greeted her eldest sister. "How does this happen?"

Lena smiled, her eyes filling with tears. "I came to see you, sister."

"Do you have time to come in?"

"Yes just let me go tell my taxi driver to come back in an hour."

"I guess I didn't realize how much I missed you!" Rose exclaimed wiping her eyes.

"Does anyone know you are here?"

"Yes. David and I talked of coming before. We want you to know that if you want to come back to the Amish church you are welcome to make your home with us."

"Thank you so much, Lena," Rose said. "You don't know how much that means to me."

"So will you come?"

"I don't know. There are just so many things about all our rules that don't make sense. Do they make sense to you?"

Lena shook her head. "No not all of them, but I understand the principle. The ministers make the rules to act as a fence to keep the world out. They are trying to make a world that is safe for us and our children."

"I understand what you are saying. But what about the things that the fence can't keep out? Like pride, anger and unforgiveness?"

"Well all I know is the fence works if you use it," Lena said gently. "Sure it has some holes, but we have to be wise enough not to go through them. Our security is inside the fence."

"Yes, but what about our salvation?" asked Rose. "What do you think it takes to get to heaven?"

"I know what you are asking. You want to know if I feel that I am saved. I have asked Jesus to come into my heart, and every day I try to live a life that is pleasing to him. Since I can't keep every commandment perfectly, I can only hope in my salvation. Don't you miss your dresses and your covering?" Lena asked changing the subject.

"Yes, sometimes. Being Amish is still a big part of who I am," Rose admitted.

"Are you ready to throw it all away?"

"I'm glad I grew up Amish. I don't like everything about it. But most of it is good."

"It's time for me to go," said Lena looking at the clock. "Will you please promise to think about coming back?"

Rose nodded. "Do you think all families in the community are like ours?"

"No. I know they are not! Please don't throw out your faith because of one person."

"I can't tell you how much it means to me that you cared enough to come see me," said Rose hugging her sister goodbye. "Can we keep in touch?"

"Yes but it will have to be done secretly. You know how strict the rules are!"

"Yes, I know how it is. Are there a lot of bad rumors going around about me?"

"A new one every week," Lena grinned. You know how gossip is!"

"Yes, I know."

"I must go, but please think about coming back. Where do you want to raise your child? Certainly not in the world, at least if you come back your child will have grandparents, aunts, and uncles. Family is important and we all need each other."

Rose returned to her duties in the house, happy that her sister had come to see her. "Dear Lord, please help me know what to do," she repeated her prayer from the previous evening.

Now that Alex wanted her to leave. What else was there to do but accept Lena's offer?

"Can I have oatmeal?" asked Lacey interrupting her thoughts.

"Sure what kind do you want?" asked Rose taking her into the kitchen.

"I like the kind you make in the pan."

"You are very sweet Lacey," Rose hugged her. She was going to miss these girls.

Finishing up with breakfast dishes, Rose picked up the phone, Michelle would help her sort it all out. She groaned with disappointment when only the answering machine picked up. "This is Rose, please call me. I need to talk."

"I have to have my heart medicine, Rose." Mrs. Scott reminded her when she brought in her lunch.

"Go ahead and eat your lunch and I'll go pick it up for you."

"Who will stay with the girls?"

"I'll ask Bernie from next door. I won't be gone too long," promised Rose.

Kristen sighed as she drove past the Miller's farm. How much longer would it be until she found Rose? She had stopped at Joseph's house, he was the only one of Rose's family that Kristen knew, but he refused to give out information about his sister.

She shook her head, it just didn't make sense. The Amish people seemed to be the kindest, gentlest people, always helping each other, but when one of their own didn't abide by the rules they were cast out and completely cut off from their family.

The ringing of her cell phone drew her back to the present.

Grabbing her purse she rummaged frantically trying to locate it.

"Hello, Hello? Lane is that you?"

"Is everything ok?"

"You're on your way home?"

"I'll be home soon. I'm just on my way to pick up a prescription for Mom."

"Ok see ya soon." Kristen clicked off the phone and threw it on the seat, excited to see her brother.

"Will Rose Miller please come to the pharmacy? Rose Miller." the announcer repeated.

Kristen stopped in her tracks. Was it possible? Her heart pounded excitedly. Turning her cart around, she quickly made her way to the pharmacy.

Kristen sighed with disappointment. She'd been hoping to see the familiar dark dress and white covering but there was none in sight. "Oh well I might as well see if they have Mom's prescription ready while I'm back here." She pushed her own cart toward the counter.

"Kristen? Kristen! I can't believe it's really you!" Rose cried with delight.

"What?" Kristen looked confused.

"It's me. Rose." Rose laughed at Kristen's bewilderment.

"Rose! Wait I don't understand. You're not Amish!" And, and you're pregnant!" she threw her arms around Rose hugging her tight.

"Oh Kristen you have no idea how much I missed you!" Rose hugged her back.

"Is it- Kristen wasn't sure how to put her question into words. "I mean you and Lane- is it his?" she stumbled over the words.

Rose nodded afraid of how Kristen might react.

"I, uh wow, I don't know what to say. Are you and uh the baby ok?"

"Yes." Rose hated the awkwardness.

"Why didn't you tell me?"

"I was scared." confessed Rose. "I was afraid of what Lane would say."

"Oh Rose I'm so sorry you had to go through this alone. Is there anything I can do? Is it a boy or girl? How much longer do have to go? You look great! You look like you have a little basket ball under your shirt." Kristen hugged her again.

Rose smiled happily. "I'm so glad you aren't mad at me."

"I could never be mad at you, silly, you're my best friend!"

"That's good."

"Were you planning on telling Lane?"

"Yes. I just didn't know when or how and I am afraid to tell him."

"He is coming home today. Shall I tell him?"

"Oh would you?" Rose begged.

The two exchanged phone numbers promising to talk later that day.

Chapter Twenty-One

"You will never guess who I ran into this afternoon when I went to get your grandmother's medicine. I ran into Kristen!" she smiled excitedly, not waiting for his response.

"Who's Kristen?"

"Kristen is my best friend and she is also Lane's sister. She went away to college, so I never knew how to get in touch with her." Rose explained.

Alex watched the smile on Rose's face when she talked about Kristen. Did this mean Lane was back in the picture again? "What about Lane?" he asked.

Rose shrugged. "Kristen said she would tell him for me. I haven't thought about him. I was just worrying about what I was going to do and where I was going to go." Tears sprang to her eyes.

"What are you talking about?" asked Alex .

"I, heard what she said about how you were to nice to tell me to leave, then when I came to your office to talk to you, I heard you say you wish you could get rid of me."

"What are you talking about?" Alex looked confused.

"I overheard Mrs. Cole and then you-"

"Wait start at the beginning." Alex held up his hand. "I'm lost."

"I wasn't talking about you, Rose." Alex responded when she'd finished. "I'm guessing I was talking about Pepper. I'm not much for having a dog in the house," he admitted.

"So you don't want me to leave?" asked Rose looking up at him.

"No, I don't want you to leave," answered Alex. I think I'm falling in love with you, he wanted to say. But how could he, when they had agreed to just be friends?

"Oh, Alex, I'm so happy I could just give you a big hug!" Rose exclaimed with relief. "I can't tell you how much it means to me to hear you say that! I know that soon you won't need me, because Mrs. Scott-

Alex put up his hand to stop her. "Am I going to get my hug or not?" His green eyes held her gaze, challenging her.

Rose blushed. "I, I, just meant," her voice trailed off when Alex stepped closer.

"I'm here," he invited in a low whisper.

Her heart pounding, Rose stepped toward him and put her arms around his neck in a quick little hug. "Thank you, Alex."

"I don't want you to go," Alex said softly pulling her close, when she would've stepped back. For several seconds he held her, breathing in the scent of her skin and hair. Brushing his lips across her cheek, he thought about the sweet kiss she'd given him several weeks ago. Who had she thought she was kissing? "That night we watched the movie you fell asleep, when I tried to wake you, you kissed me. Was I the one you thought you were kissing?"

"I did?" Rose looked shocked, she dropped her eyes shyly. "I, thought I'd just dreamt it."

Alex chuckled. "So I owe you one, don't I?"

"Daddy! Telephone!" Taylor called.

"Telephone," Alex groaned. "Someday the phone won't save you," he promised.

Rose smiled sweetly. "You better go, someone needs you."

Planting a quick kiss on her forehead, Alex headed for the living room.

"I have an emergency at the hospital," he said coming back several seconds later. "I might be awhile."

"Thanks Alex, for everything. I'm glad we talked."

"We're not done yet," Alex looked at her his green eyes twinkling, leaving her with no doubt as to what he meant.

Kristen thought about Rose, all the way home. What would her parents say? She shuddered at the thought of her mother's reaction. How would she tell Lane? Pulling into the garage, she parked the car and hurried into the kitchen.

"Where's the stuff I sent you after?" asked Mrs. Nelson seeing her daughter come in empty handed.

"Oh, I forgot. It's still out in the car,' she said turning to retrace her steps.

"Where's Lane?" asked Kristen coming back several seconds later her arms full of bags.

"He's in the family room watching T.V."

"Lane!" Kristen called. "How does it happen you could come home?"

Lane hesitated, remembering how she took the news of his deployment the last time.

"Oh Lane you're going back aren't you?" Kristen moaned.

Lane nodded. "I'm sorry. But hey, it'll be ok. I came home safe last time right?"

"I know it's just that well its different now."

"How's it different? What are you talking about?"

"I found Rose." Kristen announced unable to keep it to herself a moment longer.

"Really? How?"

"I ran into her when I was picking up Mom's prescription. Only I didn't know who she was at first."

"Why's that?" asked Lane curiously.

"Well for starters she's not Amish anymore. Remember what we talked about at Christmas time?"

Lane nodded feeling tense.

"Lane," Kristen lowered her voice to a whisper. "She is pregnant."

Lane stuffed his hands in his pockets and walked over to the window. "Are you sure?"

"Sure of what? That she's pregnant or that it's yours?" Kristen asked.

Lane shrugged. "How can I be sure?"

"Don't even go there!" Kristen sounded angry. "Do you have any idea what this has cost her? What she has been through? You better man up and do the right thing." said Kristen slamming the door as she left the room.

"Hi Rose," Kristen spoke into the phone. "It's so nice to call you whenever I want!"

"Yes, it's great!" agreed Rose.

"I was wondering when we could get together?"

"How about tomorrow I have the afternoon off."

"Sure. I was wondering if you would be willing to see Lane?" asked Kristen.

"I suppose I should. It's just well I get nervous just thinking about it."

Chapter Twenty-Two

"I'm getting together with Lane this afternoon," Rose announced as Alex was leaving for work the following morning.

Alex stopped. "Did he contact you?"

"No, Kristen told him, so he asked if we could meet."

"Did she say why he wants to meet?" Alex asked.

"No."

"Please be careful, Rose." Beware, he felt like adding. He's already proved he's a jerk.

"Please pray for me, Alex." Rose requested.

"I will," he promised.

Rose stood before her closet trying to decide what to wear. What did it matter anyhow? She would still feel huge and awkward. Michelle had advised her to wear whatever she felt most comfortable in. Though she highly doubted any dress could help her feel comfortable at this point! Deciding on a pair of jeans and black tee shirt, Rose hurried to get dressed. Putting her hair in a pony tail, she stepped in front of the mirror to check her reflection. "It doesn't matter what he thinks," she said aloud not feeling as sure of that as she wished. She thought about all the years the very thought of Lane made her heart flutter. There was something about him that had drawn her. His quest for adventure and his self assured manner had a way of promising excitement. "That was then this is now," Rose said taking one last peek in the mirror.

"I guess I'm as ready as I'll ever be," she sighed. "Dear Lord, Please be with me. Help me to know the right things to say and please help me to act in such a way that Lane could see you in me." Feeling calmer after her prayer, Rose grabbed her purse and a light sweater and headed out the door.

The small coffee house was nearly empty, observed Rose as she took a seat by a window table. I wonder what he wants; she rearranged her tea cup on her platter for the fifth time glad her table was a bit higher than the rest aiding in helping her feel like she could hide her very pregnant tummy.

Rose felt her stomach tie in knots as she thought about how badly her last encounter with Lane had ended, rejected and humiliated. Not today, she resolved. Today she would assure Lane she and the baby were fine without him.

A sleek black mustang pulled to the curb outside, and Rose watched as Lane stepped out and made his way toward the door. A fitted black tee shirt and blue jeans showed off his muscular six foot frame. If he was uncomfortable with the situation he certainly didn't show it. A credit to his military training, thought Rose.

Moments later, coffee in hand, Lane approached her table. "Hey, glad you could make it," he set his coffee down and slid into the seat across from her.

"Sure." Rose toyed with her napkin feeling awkward, finding it hard to look at Lane.

"I never meant for this to happen," Lane took a sip of his coffee.

"Me neither," Rose agreed.

"So is this why you're not Amish?"

"Yes."

A long silence followed. Rose stirred her tea. Should she just come right out and let him know he was off the hook? It was obvious that was what he wanted to hear.

"I know you were raised; the guy always marries the girl in a situation like this, right?"

"I, uh, yes, I guess so," answered Rose.

"I hope you know- I mean I can't marry you. I have my career in the military and getting married would really screw things up."

Rose looked across the table her face turning red. "I am not asking you nor would I ever want to marry you Lane. Speaking of screwing things up, what do you think my night with you has cost me?"

"So what do you want?"

"You're the one that asked for this meeting." Rose glared across the table.

"I wanted to come to an agreed price for child support, so I don't have to go through court," said Lane. "I don't expect you do this alone. I was there too."

"I don't want any money from you, Lane. I am perfectly capable of providing a life for myself and my child." Rose pushed her chair back and stood. "I hope that eases your mind."

Lane stood too. "I came to do my duty."

"Mission accomplished." Rose turned to leave. "Don't worry I won't take you to court. I know you think I'm a dumb Amish girl but I can take care of the baby myself! I'm-" a sharp searing pain shot through her abdomen causing her to stop and clutch the chair in front of her.

"Rose, I'm sorry I said that. I don't think- Are you ok?" Lane grabbed her arm.

"Please help me outside." She whispered.

The long flight of stairs to the back parking lot was her undoing.

"Could you please call Michelle? My water just broke." She choked back a sob. Why oh why did this have to happen now in front of Lane?

"I'll call the ambulance first," Lane quickly took charge. "Michelle can meet us at the hospital."

"Please don't call an ambulance," Rose protested. "I can-

Lane ignored her protests. "I am calling an ambulance. Now what is Michelle's number?"

"You're dilated to seven," the young female doctor smiled. "You should be ready to deliver shortly. I know the baby is a couple weeks early but everything seems fine so you just rest between contractions if you can."

"Are you doing ok?" Is there anything I can get you?" Lane asked when they were alone again.

Rose shook her head. "Thanks anyway. You don't have to stay. I mean-

Another contraction began and Rose was forced to leave her sentence unfinished grabbing the hand Lane offered and gripping it tightly.

"That was pretty rough," Lane commented wiping her forehead shall I go get the doctor?" He hated feeling so helpless.

"I don't know." Rose tried to regain her composure. "Thank you for staying."

Lane was spared an answer as the next contraction began. Another contraction and another on top of the last, and the doctor was called back in to make preparations to deliver the baby.

"There's a lady here that says she is your birthing coach. Her name is Michelle. Shall we bring her in?" The nurse poked her head into the room.

Rose nodded and Michelle came in all smiles. "What a surprise! Just yesterday you said you could hardly wait to see your baby who knew it'd be this soon?"

Rose produced a weak smile.

"Hey your friend is here." Lane patted Rose's shoulder. "I'll wait outside.

Michelle put her hand out, "You must be Lane? Rose needs you and you won't want to miss this. This is your baby too."

"It's up to Rose."Lane glanced at Rose. "Do you want me to stay?" he asked unsure if she wanted him there.

Rose looked at Lane, reluctant to have him stay yet knowing it was the right thing to do, she nodded her consent.

Several minutes later with Michelle on one side of Rose and Lane on the other, holding her hands and cheering her on, they witnessed the miracle of birth, a precious new life entering the world.

"It's a boy!" Dr. Hall announced placing the tiny crying infant on his Mother's bosom. "He's got a good set of lungs." The doctor chuckled. "Congratulations Daddy and Mommy."

Rose stared down at her tiny son, tears rolled down her cheeks. "I can't believe I have a son. He's perfect." she kissed his velvety soft cheeks. "Thank you God." She whispered.

Lane struggled to swallow the sudden lump in his throat suprised at the sudden rush of emotions. Pregnant was one thing but this tiny baby boy so helpless- "I need to get some fresh air." he excused himself. The Dr.'s words were still ringing in his ears. "Congratulations Daddy. Daddy? How on earth am I going to explain to my dad and mom that they are grandparents?"

Stepping out into the late afternoon sunshine, Lane made his way to a quiet spot in the hospital courtyard and dialed Kristen's number.

"Hey there Lane," Kristen's voice sounded loud in his ear. "How'd your meeting with Rose go? I've been waiting forever for you to call. Please tell you did not upset her?"

"I'm afraid I did."

"Oh Lane I knew you would! Can't you ever just-"

"Wait a minute," Lane interrupted. "Do you want to know why I called or not?"

"Yes of course."

"Rose had the baby." He said, and then waited in silence for Kristen's reaction.

"What?" Kristen asked. "Rose had the baby? How did you find out?"

"I was with her." Lane smiled, enjoying Kristen's shock, when there was only silence he relayed the afternoon's events.

"Lane you're a father!" Kristen still sounded shocked. "I'm an aunt and Dad and Mom- oh boy how are ya gonna tell Mom and Dad?"

"I don't know. I was hoping you could help me with that?"

"What did you name him?" Kristen ignored his request. "How much did he weigh? Can I come right now? What hospital?"

"I don't know anything except that it's a boy."

"Well you better get back to Rose. I'll be right there," Kristen promised after obtaining the location of the hospital. "I wouldn't call Mom and Dad; you need to do this face to face."

Lane made his way back inside unsure of what his role was. "I need a plan," he muttered. "At least when I'm deployed, I know what to do." He was used to relying on his military training; proud of the status it gave him. Today his military status hadn't made a difference. In fact he now had a new title. Daddy. Deep down inside he knew even though there was no award ceremony to announce it, this would be his most important title.

"May I come in?" Kristen entered the room carrying a huge bouquet of flowers and a large balloon that proclaimed: It's a boy!

"Where is the little guy?" she looked around the room.

"He's in the nursery."

"Are you doing ok?" Kristen bent down to give her friend a hug.

"Yes, just tired."

"How much did he weigh?"

"Five pounds and four ounces."

"Would it be ok if I went and saw him?"

"Sure go ahead. I'll just be right here." Rose smiled.

Kristen smiled at Lane watching through the huge glass window of the nursery. "Congratulations," she hugged him. "Which one is he?"

"That little guy over there on the left, under the lamp," Lane pointed out his son unable to hide the emotion in his voice.

"Oh Lane He's beautiful, and so tiny. I can't wait to hold him!"

"Where have you two been?" Mrs. Nelson looked up from her stack of paper work.

"Is Dad here?" Lane ignored her question. He was anxious to get this over with. Even though he could stand eyeball to eyeball with his father, Lane found no comfort in that at the moment. At six foot and two inches, Tom Nelson, head of the Hudson county Sherriff's department was more than just a little intimidating and Lane's four years of military experience, awards and achievements could never measure up to Mr. Nelson's expectations.

"Oh that must be him now," Mrs. Nelson flipped on the garage light. "There was a retirement dinner for Mrs. Johnson so he's running a little late."

"How was the party Dad?" asked Kristen.

"It was ok." He set his briefcase on the table.

"What's wrong with you two?" He scrutinized Lane and Kristen.

"How does he do that?" Kristen muttered getting a pop from the fridge.

Lane knew his father expected the truth the whole truth and nothing less.

Gathering up his courage, Lane dived in, "I slept with a girl last summer and then on Saturday when I came home I found out that she was pregnant."

Mr. and Mrs. Nelson stood in silent shock for several long seconds.

"I know I made a mistake," Lane apologized, hating to be wrong, especially in front of his father.

"No son leaving your car lights on is a mistake." Mr. Nelson responded sarcastically.

"Do we know the girl? Are you sure she's pregnant?" Mrs. Nelson questioned.

"I, ah, yes you know her and Kristen and I just came from the hospital. She had the baby this afternoon."

Chapter Twenty-Three

"Knock. Knock." Alex called from the doorway. "Is it ok if I come in?"

"Alex what a nice surprise!" Rose smiled.

"How are you feeling?" Alex came over to bed and bent down to hug her.

"I feel great." Rose returned his hug. "I hope I didn't make too much trouble for you. It was probably hard to find someone for the girls at such short notice."

Alex pulled a chair up to the bed. "No, you didn't make too much trouble."

"Oh that's good."

"How did things go with Lane yesterday?"

"Oh Alex I was so mad! He wanted to make sure I wasn't expecting him to marry me."

Alex covered his mouth with his hand to hide his grin. He could well imagine Rose's indignation.

"And then when I was about to make my dramatic exit this horrible pain started in my stomach and he had to help me outside and he was here for the whole thing."

"What was-

"Are you ready for a hungry little boy?" interrupted the nurse bringing in a crying little bundle. "I'm sorry I didn't know you had company. Oh it's you Dr. Scott."

"Hey Mrs. Riley, how are you this morning?" Alex took the baby from her. "I haven't gotten to see this little guy yet."

"Oh he's a doll. We've all been fightin' over him in the nursery."

"I can see why. He's a handsome little guy."

"I wish my Mom could see him, she loved seeing her new grandchildren." Rose felt the pain of regret at what would not be.

"You mean she won't come see him?" Alex looked surprised.

"Anybody home?" Kristen tapped on the door.

"Come in," Rose called. "Kristen, this is my friend Alex. He came to check up on us."

"Hi nice to meet you. You must be this little guy's aunt?"

"Yes and I haven't even gotten to hold him yet." Kristen held out her arms. "Is it ok if I steal him?"

"Sure. I've got to get goin' anyway. It was nice meeting you Kristen." Alex handed her the baby and turned to Rose. "Please be sure and let me know if you need anything."

"I brought Lane's baby pictures to show you how much your baby looks like Lane did as a baby." Kristen dug in her purse to get the photographs.

"So did you guys tell your Mom and Dad about the baby?"

"Yes Lane told them last night."

"What was their reaction?"

"Um not to good at first." Kristen admitted. "You know what perfectionists they are. God forbid that they should be made to look bad." She rolled her eyes in exasperation. "How much longer will you be in here?"

"I'm not going home till tonight."

"Where are you going?"

"My friend Michelle said I could stay at their house."

"Did you decide on a name yet?" Kristen asked.

"I like the name Joshua."

"Are you naming him after anyone?"

"No. At first I couldn't make up my mind what to name him, and then my friend Michelle said that I should pray and ask God what to name him. I wasn't sure if I wanted to do that or not," Rose admitted. "I was afraid maybe God would tell me to name him something I didn't like."

"Do you really think God cares what you name your baby?"

"Yes. God created him, so of course He cares," said Rose.

"So how did you decide on Joshua?"

"Well I was taught to believe that you have to be perfect to get to heaven, and that I had to be Amish. I thought about what I want my son to remember and that is why I picked the name Joshua because it means: God is my salvation." Rose took baby Joshua and prepared to feed him.

"Do you have a middle name picked out?"

"I thought Lane would be nice, but I didn't know if Lane would want that."

"Oh Rose would you really be willing to do that?"

"Yes. I won't keep Lane from Joshua. I assumed he wouldn't want anything to do with him."

"I don't think he knows how he feels. Last night, when I went to the nursery to see Joshua, I found Lane standing there just watching him."

Rose was silent for several moments, as she concentrated on getting Joshua to eat. "I guess I have to remember I had almost nine months to get used to the idea."

"Yes I think it's safe to say he's still in shock, along with Mom and Dad." Kristen began giggling hysterically. "Can you imagine what it was like for my mom and dad to find out they were grandparents? Dad is always doing some kind of detective work and Mom is always helping other people solve their problems. She prides herself with all her degrees in psychology."

Rose laughed too. "It feels good to laugh with you again. I have really missed you."

"I missed you too. I dread thinking about how much I'm gonna miss Lane."

"Where is Lane going?"

"Oh, didn't I tell you? He's being deployed to Iraq."

"You must be scared for him."

"Yes especially now. I don't want Joshua to grow up without a Daddy."

"I guess I didn't think about that."

"Hey the guy that was here when I got here is he your doctor?" asked Kristen.

"No. Alex is the guy I work for."

"You never mentioned he was so cute."

"I didn't have time, there were too many other things to tell you about."

"Is he available or does he have a brother?" Kristen asked jokingly.

"Actually he does have a brother that's a missionary in Europe."

"I just don't know about all that God and church stuff." Kristen shrugged.

"I know I used to feel that way too, so if you ever have any questions I'll try and tell you what I know." Rose offered.

Lane hesitated, the door to Rose's room stood ajar, should he call out or knock? Stepping closer, he looked inside. Seated in the corner of the room was Rose, head slightly bent talking intently to baby Joshua. Lane drew back, he knew the scene he had just witnessed, was much like the worn paper photographs his army buddies carried, it would stay fixed in his memory. "I don't need that kind of drama," he muttered to himself.

Reaching out he knocked lightly. "Can I come in?"

"Sure. I didn't know you were coming."

"I'm not interrupting am I?"

"No we were just talking." Rose smiled down at Joshua her face glowing. "See he's looking at me."

"Really?"

"Sure. I think he knows I'm his mommy." Rose smiled proudly. "Oh Lane isn't he the most beautiful baby you ever saw?"

"He is, but I've never been around babies." Lane looked down at Joshua.

"I didn't think about that." Rose fingered the edge of Joshua's blanket, wishing it wouldn't be so awkward between them.

"I brought him something," Lane held out a teddy bear dressed in Army clothes.

"Oh that's so cute. Look Joshua at what your Daddy brought -" Rose stopped short. "I uh maybe I shouldn't have said that?" she apologized. "What I mean is I don't know if you even want….."

"It's ok," Lane interrupted. "I'm not sure how I feel. I don't know what I'm supposed to do," He shifted uncomfortably.

"You don't have to do anything." Rose replied. "It's up to you if you want him in your life. I'm not going to keep him from you, nor am I going to push him on you."

"I just need some time to, - to adjust to the fact that I have a son."

"I understand. It was a hard process for me too. Sometimes I wished I could wake up and the whole thing would've been just a dream. But now that he's here and he looks at me with those big brown eyes, I love him more than I ever knew it was possible to love anyone." Rose smoothed her hand over Joshua's thick black hair.

"Well I just came to say goodbye," Lane said. "Do you mind if I hold him?"

"No I don't mind," Rose stood and handed him baby Joshua. "I'll just take a little walk and give you some time alone with him."

"You don't have to do that," Lane protested.

"Go ahead." Rose smiled. "I'll be back in a few minutes."

Lane looked down at the tiny newborn he was holding. Big bright eyes stared back at him. "I'm sorry I don't know what I'm doing. I'm sure you can tell." He felt strange talking to a baby. "You're so little," He touched his hand. "Your hands are the size of my thumb." Lane placed his thumb on Joshua's hand. "What's this? Your name tag?" said Lane sliding the tiny bracelet around to read the lettering. Joshua Lane Miller. Lane couldn't suppress the emotion he felt. "I didn't know she did that. Did you?"

In response to Lane's question, Joshua yawned tiredly and clutched Lane's thumb. Lane stared at the tiny fingers wrapped around his thumb, his mind went back to when he was seven and climbed the ladder to find his father on the garage roof. He was several feet away from his father when he slipped and began sliding but just before he went over the edge, his father grabbed his hand. Lane remembered that moment; his hand being the little hand hanging onto his father's for dear life. Now his hand was the father's hand.

Lane walked over to the window and stared out into the afternoon sunshine. In three days, he would be worlds away in the hot desert sun, a soldier fighting for his country. "What are you doing to me? All I came to do was say goodbye."

Rose wandered down the hall to the hospital chapel and slipped inside, grateful it was empty so she could be alone. Closing the door behind her she knelt on the floor. "Dear God, I feel so overwhelmed." She prayed feeling the weight of this new responsibility. How was she going to care for Joshua alone? There were so many things about babies she didn't know, and now she wouldn't have her own mom to help her. How was she going to work to provide and take care of Joshua? "Please help me Father. I need wisdom to be a good mom."

Rose got up and took a seat overlooking the hospital garden thinking about how much her life had changed in the past two days. She thought about all the little things that had mattered to her before, but looking at Joshua's little face changed everything. He was all that mattered now. "Thank you God for a healthy baby. Thank you that you have provided for me these past few months," Rose whispered her prayer thinking about the many blessings God had given her. Peace began to fill her heart. God was with her. It was going to be ok.

"I'm back," Rose took a seat on the edge of the bed. "Kristen left her camera here. "Shall I take a picture?"

"Sure." Lane carefully shifted Joshua to face the camera.

Rose felt her heart soften toward Lane as she seen the vulnerability in his eyes.

"I'll tell Kristen to send these to you." Rose snapped several pictures. "If you want, that is?"

Lane nodded, "That would be nice. Hey, about the other day - I'm sorry"

"Me too." Rose fingered the edge of the pillow. "Thanks for coming with me."

"I hate this," Lane ran his hands through his hair. "I grew up with you, we were friends and now I – my whole world has changed."

"What are you trying to say?"

"That's just it. I always know where I'm going and what I'm doing," Lane said.

Rose came to stand beside him. "I don't know what I'm doing either. I look at Joshua and I just want everything to be perfect for him. I'm just asking God to help me. We will have to learn just like everyone else."

"I suppose you're right," Lane turned to face her. "Thanks for letting me see him."

"Thanks for coming. Be careful Lane. I'll pray for your safe return."

"Thanks," Lane carefully handed her baby Joshua, then leaned forward and hugged her, before exiting the room.

"I can't tell you how much it means to me that you are taking me in again!" Rose thanked Michelle.

"Rose you are part of our family."

"We missed you." Melissa took a seat beside her on the sofa.

"I missed you too." Rose reached over and tugged her pony tail.

"Did you miss me too?" Jaden crowded between them.

"Yes of course I did." Rose pinched his cheek.

"Ok children, you go play so Rose can feed Joshua and put him down for a nap."

"So how did things go between you and Lane?" Michelle asked curiously after the children left the room.

"He was pretty stressed out. He just found out he has a son, plus he's leaving tomorrow for Iraq."

"That would definitely be a lot to deal with." Michelle agreed. "How are his parents reacting?"

"Not too good. It's certainly not what they dreamed of for Lane. They are afraid they will be made to look bad. However, I am invited to their house tomorrow evening. They want to see the baby."

"How do feel about that?"

"I'm dreading it. I am ashamed to face them."

"Just give then some time to adjust." Michelle advised.

"You are looking so handsome; your grandpa Nelson's are not going to be able to resist you." Kristen cooed to Joshua as she fastened him into his car seat.

"I hope you're right." Rose slid into the front seat. "Thanks for coming to pick us up. Michelle wouldn't let me drive."

"And she's right. You should wait at least two weeks. Goodness you just had a baby, although you would never know it by the looks of you!"

"I'm glad; I was worried I might never be thin again. But now, I have nothing to wear that fits me."

"I have some things for you, and I would love to take you shopping."

"Oh that sounds like fun. I'm looking forward to spending time with you."

"Listen, Mom and Dad were pretty shocked by this whole thing so just give them some time to get used to the idea." Kristen advised as they pulled into the garage.

"I understand."

"We're back," Kristen announced as they entered the kitchen.

"We're in the living room honey," Mrs. Nelson responded. "Come on in here."

Rose clutched Joshua tighter, wanting desperately to turn around and run out of the house, much like she had nearly nine months ago.

Mr. and Mrs. Nelson rose when the girls entered.

"Hi Rose," Mr. Nelson offered a rather stiff greeting. "I understand you brought our grandson to show us."

Rose felt intimidated under his stare. "Yes I have." She forced herself to return his gaze.

"May I hold him?" Mrs. Nelson held out her perfectly manicured hands.

"Sure," Rose handed over her little son, waiting anxiously for her reaction.

Mrs. Nelson took a seat and pulled back the blanket. "Oh Tom," she gasped "he looks just like Lane did when he was a baby!"

Mr. Nelson bent down to have a look. "Yes he does."

Rose watched and listened as they examined and discussed baby Joshua. She cleared her throat nervously gathering up her courage, "I know this was not uh what you wanted. I mean, not how you wanted things for Lane and I'm sorry," she forced herself to look them both in the eye.

"Thank you Rose." Mr. Nelson responded. "I appreciate that."

"This has all come as such a shock to us." Mrs. Nelson kept her eyes on Joshua.

"I understand," Rose said apologetically.

"Do you want to go up to my room to look at the clothes I have for you?"

"Sure that would be great." Rose stood an offered to take Joshua.

"You girls go ahead. I think I can handle holding a sleeping baby." Mrs. Nelson replied not taking her eyes off her new grandson.

Chapter Twenty-Four

"Your sister Lena sent a message that you are invited to come to their house for lunch." Michelle announced several days later. "Michael stopped in at their house this morning to give David a ride to town. He said Lena and the girls were full of questions about you."

"Oh that will be so nice. I will finally get to show someone in my family my baby."

Everything was just as Rose expected when she arrived at David and Lena's house. Six little girls were lined up at door waiting to be the first to hold baby Joshua. There was Anna, the oldest, who at fifteen was the second mother of the house and Ruby, twelve, who was always playing tricks on her brothers and even now longed to be out in the barn with them playing with the litter of new puppies. Mary eleven, who loved writing poems, and Priscilla four, Doris, three, and Elizabeth, two, who played with their dolls every waking moment.

"Can I be first to hold him?" begged Doris.

"Me too. Me too." chimed in Elizabeth stretching out her chubby little arms.

"You can all have a turn," Rose smiled. "Maybe we should start with Anna, since she is the oldest," said Rose handing Joshua to Anna and taking a seat on the hickory rocker. "It's so *gute* to be here."

"Oh he's so tiny," Anna exclaimed removing Joshua's blankets. "He's half the size Jonas was." She said referring to her youngest brother.

Rose sat back and watched with great enjoyment, all the fussing over Joshua. She felt again a pang of regret that Mom and Katie couldn't be present.

"I never knew babies ate so often," Rose moaned once she found a moment alone with Lena "I think I fed him every hour during the night last night."

Lena laughed. "The first couple weeks can be rough."

"I'm worried about being a single parent. I don't even know how to be a parent at all," the tears began rolling down her cheeks. "I feel like crying all the time."

"Ah you have a case of baby blues," Lena nodded wisely as she explained the condition to Rose. "See, that is why family is so important," she concluded.

"I guess maybe I let my bitterness toward Dad make me forget that," admitted Rose. "It's been so nice to see your family. You and David get along, and he is not harsh or unreasonable with the children."

"Yah, I appreciate him. He is a *gute* husband and father."

"How is everyone at home?" Rose changed the subject. "Do Mom or Katie ever talk about me?"

" Yes, if Dad is not around. Poor Katie really misses you. Oh wait, you probably have not heard about Katie?"

"Heard what?"

"Remember Dad's friend Marvin Chupp?"

"The guy that lost his wife a year or two back?"

"Yes that's him. He came to ask Dad for Katie!" Lena whispered in an angry hushed tone. "Can you believe his nerve? He's twenty five years older than Katie! "Please tell me Dad said no?"

Lena shook her head. "Marvin is a deacon too, and Dad thinks Katie should be honored. And you know Katie; she would think it a sin to ever say no to Dad."

"Surely there is something we can do to- to get her out of that situation." Rose felt her anger toward her father boiling inside her. "Oh Lena, sometimes I think I'm doing really good and that I have forgiven Dad, but right now I am so angry at him!"

"Yah I know." Lena agreed. "I have struggled with anger toward Dad for years."

"Michelle has taught me that we must continue to forgive. We cannot just say we forgive someone once and then expect to feel love for that person, she says that it's a process."

"It certainly has been a battle for me!" agreed Lena. "Maybe Michelle is right.

"Today we are going to church," Rose smiled at Joshua as she buttoned up his outfit. "You will be the best looking baby there!" she bent down and kissed his nose.

Rose checked her reflection one last time. "I just need a little blush and then I will be ready," She said to Joshua. "You're mama has to look pretty too."

"Mommy said she is ready to go," Melissa knocked on the door.

"I'll be right there." answered Rose fumbling with her makeup box. "I'm glad I may wear makeup," she muttered, "I just wish I knew how."

"You look great," Michelle complimented. "I love that white skirt."

"Does my makeup look ok?" worried Rose.

"I didn't know you had any on," laughed Michelle.

"I put on some blush."

"If you ever need any help with it I can show you what I know."

"Going to church with you today is so different than it would've been if I would've still been Amish." Rose said once everyone was belted in and on their way.

"How so?"

"Well most of the people would've been kind, but some of the people would've been very condescending. They would act in such a way as to make sure that every young girl in the community would know the shame of having a child out of wedlock. I still struggle with shame," admitted Rose. "Even though the day would have come when I would be accepted as a member again, I would still never quite be accepted by most of the people. I would be kind of an outcast and so would Joshua."

"Does that help you not to feel such a pull to go back?" wondered Michelle.

"I still miss everyone, but I know that because I have changed so much even if I did go back, it wouldn't be the same."

"Will you ever be able to have a relationship with your parents again?"

"Only if I went back and became a part of the church again."

The arrival at the church brought the conversation to a close as Michelle and Rose took the children from the van and herded their little group inside to their perspective Sunday school classrooms.

"Thanks for helping me with the kids," said Michelle. "I still struggle so much with wanting to be independent. I was so used to doing everything myself and now," Michelle's voice choked.

Rose reached over and squeezed her hand. "You are doing great, Michelle. You have come a long way since the first day I met you. Not so?" Rose reverted back to an old Amish phrase.

Michelle nodded.

"I know I can't begin to imagine how you must feel, but one thing you taught me is when I am hurting I should focus on something I am thankful for. Today, we are thankful that you are here for your children."

Michelle took a deep breath to compose herself. "Thank you Rose. You are right."

"I know I am, because you taught me and it works." Rose grinned

Michelle smiled back brushing a tear from her cheek. "Michael is leading worship today. Would you mind sitting with me?"

"I would love to." agreed Rose.

Alex adjusted the piano bench and organized his music sheets. "I probably shouldn't have agreed to do this," he muttered. "I'm too rusty, I haven't played much since Caitlin's gone." He ran his fingers softly over the keys.

"Still got it." Michael nodded. "I wish I had you in here every Sunday."

"Oh I don't know about that but I do miss it," Alex played a few chords.

"I heard about your Dad-

"Hey Michael," the drummer called. "Got a minute?"

"We'll talk after?"

Alex nodded. "Sounds good." He got up to adjust his microphone.

"Do want to go out for lunch with us?" Michelle asked Rose after church.

"Sure, that sounds nice. Shall I go get the children from their classes?"

"My mom and dad are taking them for the afternoon."

"You two go ahead without me, you and Michael could use some time alone."

"That's ok. Michael invited Alex too. Alex has something he wants to talk about."

"Well," Rose hesitated.

"I won't take no for an answer." Alex joined them. "My treat."

"In that case I will come," agreed Rose returning Alex's smile.

"Tell us what's on your mind?" Michael looked at Alex once they were seated.

"I got a call from my Mom yesterday." Alex said. "My dad was diagnosed with pancreatic cancer."

"Oh, I'm sorry." Michael laid a hand on Alex's shoulder. "Brings back a lot of memories huh?"

Alex nodded the pain evident in his face.

"I'm sorry, Alex." Rose said

"Are you going out there to visit him?" asked Michelle.

"Well that's the thing, Mom would like me to come and stay a few months and help her with Dad's practice. She would like me to move there permanently of course. I do want to go for awhile, but I'm just not sure how I would make arrangements for my own practice."

"You would probably have a much better income if you took over your dad's practice?" Michael asked.

"Yes, it would take me years to be able to build my business here to the kind of income my dad makes."

"Where are the girls?" asked Michelle.

"Aunt Cheryl took them along with her daughters to a birthday party."

"Have you talked to the Taylor and Lacey yet?" asked Rose.

"No, I am just trying to sort it all out."

"Is everyone ready to order?" their waitress appeared tablet in hand.

"Are we all ok with the brunch buffet?" Alex looked around at everyone.

"Sounds good to me." Michael rubbed his stomach.

"You and Michael go ahead." Alex nodded toward the buffet. "I'll go with Rose after you come back."

"You look great," Alex smiled at Rose after Michael and Michelle left the table.

"Thanks, I feel great."

"Have you decided what you're going to do?"

"I talked to Mrs. Wilmer again yesterday. Her mother is coming this week and she offered me her basement apartment for the summer in exchange to come and help care for her mother while she is there. I plan to move in on Thursday."

"That sounds nice. I was hoping, if you're not too busy, maybe you and I could spend some time together."

"I would like that." Rose admitted.

"I think we have some unfinished business," Alex said very softly.

Rose felt herself blushing under Alex's intimate gaze. "I don't know what you're talking about."

"That's ok. I'll remind you." Alex chuckled mischievously.

"Rose is that you?" A voice spoke up in line behind her as she reached for the french toast.

"Yes," answered Rose more cheerfully than she felt turning to greet Mrs. Nelson.

"We are here with my brother and his wife. Would it be possible for you to bring Joshua over to the table so we can introduce him to them?"

"Sure, I'll bring him over as soon as I finish eating."

"Thanks. Um, Rose what have you told people about you and Lane?" Mrs. Nelson struggled with her words.

"I haven't even told my own family that Lane is the father of my child." Rose said.

"Oh, we just aren't sure what to tell people," Mrs. Nelson said.

"We don't have to tell them anything." Rose said gently having a moment of compassion. "Tell them to pray for Lane's safety and then ask him when he comes home."

"Thank you for- for understanding." Mrs. Nelson busied herself with pouring syrup over her waffles.

"Its ok." Rose turned and headed back toward the table.

"Sorry, I didn't wait on you." Alex smiled apologetically when she arrived at the table. "I seen you were talking to someone and I didn't want to interrupt."

"It was Mrs. Nelson. She asked if I could bring Joshua over to their table."

"How do you feel about that?" asked Michelle.

"Annoyed. I am trying to be a single parent and all she is worried about is what other people think."

Chapter Twenty-Five

"So how did the introduction of the baby go?" asked Michelle.

"Ok I guess, while I was there Mrs. Nelson said she thought two weeks from today would be a good time for the baby shower." Rose rolled her eyes.

"Did you know they were planning a baby shower?"

"No."

"Do they want you and Lane to get married?"

"No. I just know this has been a source of shame for them, and I do feel bad about it," Rose said.

"What if Lane had a change of heart and would want to marry you?" Michelle sipped her too hot coffee.

"I certainly don't see that happening."

"I know this is a lot to think about, but someday Joshua will want a daddy."

Rose toyed with her napkin. "I guess I never thought about that."

"I think that's the last of it." Kristen announced as she set the stack of boxes in the middle of the floor. "Is this really all of your belongings?"

"I don't need much for just me and Joshua." laughed Rose.

"I know you are going to be living here in exchange for helping Mrs. Wilmer take care of her mother but what are you going to do for money like paying for your groceries and gas for your car?" worried Kristen.

"I have a couple houses to clean every week, because I won't be needed here fulltime. I will make enough that way."

"Do you make good money cleaning houses?"

"Yes and when I clean Michelle's house, I can take Joshua along so I won't have to pay a babysitter."

"I would love to help out with Joshua too." said Kristen.

"Thanks, I'm sure there will be times when I need help."

"I should probably run," Kristen glanced at her watch. "I'm supposed to help mom get ready for your baby shower."

"I really feel bad that she is doing all this. I mean I know she is ashamed of this whole situation."

"Don't feel bad. Mom just needs to stop living her whole life according to what everyone else thinks." Kristen slung her purse over her shoulder. "I do feel inclined to warn you that mom has some pretty snooty friends and family."

"What shall I do?" worried Rose.

"Be yourself and don't care what they think." advised Kristen.

"Michelle what does a person wear to a baby shower?" Rose pinched her cell phone between her ear and shoulder as she looked through her clothes.

"I think you could wear those white capri's and one of your new tops and those new sandals you got last week." advised Michelle.

"I wish you could go with me. I feel scared to go alone."

"You will be ok. Remember call and tell me all about it when you get home."

Rose rubbed her mid section to try and ease the nervous ache as she drove in the Nelson's lane. "Lord please help me not to do or say anything stupid," she breathed a quick prayer as she parked her car.

"Oh good you're here!" Kristen came to greet her. "You look very nice."

"Oh that's good I was so worried about what to wear."

"Here's our little guest of honor." announced Mrs. Nelson taking Joshua from Rose's arms. "Isn't he the cutest baby you ever saw?"

"He looks just like Lane," great grandma Nelson said proudly.

Several other guests arrived and everyone crowded around to inspect the new addition to the Nelson clan. Happy that no one was paying any attention to her, Rose slipped out to the kitchen to get a soda.

"I was hoping I could find a quiet moment alone with you," said Mrs. Nelson. "Can I be really up front with you?"

"Sure." Rose agreed. "What is it you want to tell me?"

"Well I was wondering if we could keep the fact that you used to be Amish our little secret?"

"I uh sure." Rose mumbled her face turning red with embarrassment.

"I just think the less people know about the situation the better," Mrs. Nelson reached over and patted Roses' hand. "I'm sure you feel that way too."

The arrival of several more guests at that precise moment spared Rose from having to answer. Seeing her chance to escape Rose slipped into the bathroom and locked the door. They are ashamed of me; she fought back her tears wishing she could grab Joshua and disappear.

"Rose," Kristen knocked on the door. "Where's your diaper bag? Joshua is ready for a diaper change."

"I'll be right there." Rose took a deep breath. "I can do this for you Joshua. I have no reason to be ashamed that I was Amish."

"So how did you and Lane meet?" asked Aunt Julie Thompson when everyone gathered to watch Rose open the presents.

Rose paused in the middle of the gift she was unwrapping, knowing every ear was tuned waiting for her answer, anxious to unravel the mystery of who she was. "Lane and I have known each other since first grade," she answered hiding a smile at the thought of Mrs. Nelson's relief.

Rose unwrapped the next gift, hoping there would be no further questions.

"I realized today more than ever just how much I don't fit in," Rose moaned to Michelle over a cup of coffee. "Everyone was so nicely made up, they were wearing jewelry and their nails were done. I tried to keep my hands hidden while I was unwrapping the gifts."

"I know that stuff seems so important," Michelle agreed. "And before I lost my leg I used to think so too. I'm not saying it's wrong to look nice, but we just have to check and make sure our priorities are lined up with what God's word says is important."

Rose nodded in agreement. "Oh Michelle I really needed to hear that. I hope I can learn your ways but I do not want to lose sight of what's really important."

Chapter Twenty-Six

The hot dessert sun beat down harshly, as Lane made his way to the barracks. A long grueling mission that had lasted over forty two hours had left him exhausted. Worst of all they'd lost two men. He cursed at the flies swarming around his head and dropped his rucksack outside the barracks door.

"Hey Nelson," his team leader shouted. "Let's head to the chow hall."

"I need a shower and sleep," muttered Lane angrily under his breath. Who wants to eat after all that?

"I hope they have chicken. I'm hungry for my wife's grilled chicken, this stuff tastes like crap!" complained his team leader. "You got a wife and kids?"

Lane hesitated, not sure how much information he wanted to give to the new guy. "I have a son," he finally admitted.

"But you're not married?"

"No."

"You gonna marry her when ya get back?"

Lane thought about his conversation with Rose at the coffee shop, ashamed now at his arrogance when she wasn't asking for anything. "Don't know," he replied.

"She givin' ya hassel?"

Lane shook his head, wishing he could tell his companion to shut up.

"Is she takin' ya to the cleaners for the kid?"

"I didn't know ya had kid Nelson," his roommate stepped in line behind him and grabbed a tray.

"Didn't know you were interested?" Lane kept his back turned.

"What's she got ya payin' a month? I pay six hundred a month for my kid and she ain't even a year old and then I can only see her if it's convenient!"

Lane nodded in agreement as several other guys joined in the conversation. He certainly wasn't going to let these guys know he wasn't paying child support.

Lane was silent through lunch only half listening to the other soldier stories about their kids and wives or girlfriends. He thought about the partner he'd lost less than 24 hours earlier. Zack lived for letters and phone calls from his wife and kids. "I can't wait till Zack Jr. is big enough for me to teach him how to play football, he'd say. Now, Zack's life was over at age twenty-eight. Why Zack? Why not some of these other idiots that just lived for the next party?

"Hey Nelson," Chaplin Reed approached Lane's table. "If you're done here, I'd like a word with you."

Lane got up relieved for an excuse to leave the room.

"I am very sorry that you lost your buddy Zack." Chaplin Reed expressed his sympathy once they were outside. "If you want to talk or if you have any questions-

"Yeah, maybe if you can tell me why Zack? Why not some other idiot that has no wife and kids?" Lane exploded.

Chaplin Reed nodded. "I'm sorry but I don't have an answer for you. I know there are a lot of why's in life that I don't have the answer to I just figure that someday, when I get to heaven, I'll ask God."

Lane walked in silence beside the Chaplin. Heaven. Was there such a place? "If there is a God what kind of God is he that he would let a good man die?" Lane asked angrily.

"The same God that sent His own son to die for you." Chaplin Reed looked him straight in the eye.

Lane shifted uncomfortably. These were the same words Zack had told him last week. "Dude" he'd said "I don't know what you're waitin on. We have no promise of tomorrow. You might think you're in control but come on, think back over your life, how much of it went exactly like you planned? One thing I know I can control and that is where I will spend eternity. If you think being here in this dessert where the air feels like a blow dryer set on high blowin' sand in your eyes and you are desperate for just one glimpse of or one touch from the ones you love, it ain't nothing compared to hell. You know when you are headin' back to your family, bro, you can leave this place but you can't leave hell."

"He's in a better place," Chaplain Reed said quietly. "I know that may not answer any questions or heal the pain, but maybe that thought will bring you some comfort." Sensing that Lane needed time to sort it all out, Chaplain Reed bade him good bye. "Come see me anytime," he invited.

Lane made his way back to his sleeping quarters sick from exhaustion. "Maybe a shower and a couple hours of sleep will help me sort things out," he said to himself.

"Package for ya man," Sergeant Redd tossed a box at him as he stepped into the room.

Lane caught the box and looked around for a quiet corner. A huge bag of candy, "to share" Kristen had written, a box of grandma's sugar cookies "just for you" written across the top of the box, a car magazine, a book by his favorite author, and a stack of pictures. "Joshua is getting cuter every day," Kristen had scrawled across the top of the stack.

Lane looked through the pictures. Grandma with Joshua, Grandpa with Joshua, Kristen with Joshua and last of all a picture of Rose holding Joshua smiling, Lane stared at the picture a long time. For a brief moment, he wondered what it would be like if Rose and Joshua belonged to him. An unfamiliar feeling of longing stirred an ache within him. "You can't be feeling like this," he muttered stuffing the pictures back into the envelope. "You're a soldier, you have a job to do here."

Chapter Twenty-Seven

"So what did the Doctor say?" asked Michelle as the two of them chatted on the phone.

"She said I am doing great," Rose said proudly.

"I can hardly believe Joshua is six weeks old already."

"Time has sure gone by fast," agreed Rose. "I'm sorry Michelle I got someone beeping in on my other line. Can we talk tomorrow?"

"Sure." Michelle agreed.

Rose switched to her other line.

"Hi," she pinched the phone between her ear and shoulder as she lay Joshua in his crib.

"Hey Rose," came Alex's deep voice bringing an instant smile from Rose.

"How are you?" they exchanged pleasantries.

"Are you free tomorrow night?" Alex asked.

"Sure, do you need me to watch the girls?"

"No, I was hoping to take you to dinner."

"That sounds nice."

"Would it be ok if I asked Michelle to keep our kids so it could be just the two of us?"

"Shall I ask her?" Rose offered.

"No, I have to call her anyway. How does six-thirty sound?"

"Sure shall I meet you somewhere?"

"How about we meet at Michelle's?"

"That would fine."

"See you tomorrow then?"

"Yes."

"I'm sorry to rush off Rose, but I have a dozen calls to make yet tonight," said Alex bidding her good night.

"You look beautiful," Alex came around leaned in for a quick hug and held her door open.

Rose hugged him back loving to hear his compliment. She had taken great pains to prepare for this evening, choosing a knee length soft floral print dress.

"Thanks so do you," Rose slid into the front seat of the jeep noticing Alex's appearance too. She loved his slightly messy brown hair and mischievous green eyes.

"I made reservations at the River Walk," Alex said. "I hope that's ok."

"I have never been there. It sounds nice."

"It's been a very long time since I've been on a date," Alex said.

"I've never been on one," admitted Rose.

"Really? Why?"

"I guess I never wanted to go with anyone that asked me before."

"So what would an Amish date have been like?"

"Well since I never had a date I can't be completely sure, but I do have a funny story about a date my sister had," Rose laughed.

"I love your stories," Alex said.

"Well this one particular guy had brought my sister Esther home several times, so Esther decided to try and impress him. She spent all of Saturday evening baking her special yellow chiffon cake. She was such a perfectionist."

"Where did they have their date?" Alex interrupted.

"It was summer and so Esther decided to bring this guy around to the sun porch. It was so much more romantic than the kitchen table. She gave Katie and I strict orders to make sure the porch was clean and a fresh bouquet of flowers were on the table in her best vase. She set a couple little lamps on the side tables then she cut two big slices of the cake and covered them with the frosting she made and put them in a basket in the basement."

"Why did she put them in the basement?"

"It was the only way to keep it cool. We didn't have a refrigerator. We did have an ice chest but that was for cooling milk." explained Rose. "Well that Sunday afternoon after she left Katie and I decided to play a trick on Esther. We took some leftover cornbread and frosted it with some of Esther's delicious homemade frosting and then we made the switch." Rose giggled at the memory.

"What happened?" Alex asked enjoying Rose's story.

"We made sure the lamps were lit and the flowers were in place. We could hardly wait until the next morning to get her reaction. We weren't disappointed either! According to Esther, after several minutes of small talk she served her cake and some of mom's special raspberry sun tea. She was so nervous she only licked a bit of the frosting, it wasn't till after he went home that she settled down on the swing to eat her piece and that's when she discovered she'd fed her date cornbread!" Rose laughed hysterically. "She said he complimented her on the frosting and said that any cake was worth eating just for the frosting!"

"Did he ever ask her out again?"

"Yes, he married her two years later, but she still doesn't see the humor in it." Rose

laughed.

"You sure have a very mischievous side," chuckled Alex.

"Not true." denied Rose smiling.

"This is so beautiful," Rose looked around the restaurant. "I've never been anywhere this nice." She said as she took in the cathedral ceilings, the beautiful tables, and soft lighting that caught sparkles of light from the fine crystal dinnerware.

"I'm glad you like it. What are you hungry for?"

"I can't make up my mind," Rose put the menu down feeling too embarrassed that she did not know what many of the items were that were listed.

"Shall I order for us?"

"That would be nice."

"I can tell you have something on your mind Alex?" observed Rose as they waited for their food to arrive.

Alex toyed with his fork. "It's been a rough couple weeks. I've had to make some hard decisions."

"Do want to talk about it?"

"Let's wait till after dinner and then we can take a walk around the lake and have a little more privacy."

"Thanks so much for bringing me," Rose said as they made their way outside to the beach after dinner.

"I've enjoyed every minute."

"Me too."

"Remember how I said earlier that it's been a hard couple weeks?"Alex asked.

"Did you decide to move?" asked Rose.

"Yes. I spent a lot of time praying about it. I know it's what God wants me to do, but," Alex didn't finish his sentence.

"It's hard to make such a big change," Rose sympathized.

"Yes, even though there are some positive things about it. The girls will have grandparents around all the time and I will have my family too."

The two walked in silence several moments.

"I am very glad I met you Rose," Alex reached over and took her hand. "You have brought so many good changes to my life. Before you came along I was just burying myself in my work to get away from the pain of losing Caitlin. All I saw when I looked at the future was me alone. I never imagined I could ever let anyone in my heart again." Alex stopped and looked at Rose. "I feel different now. I feel like I could love again, and I want it to be you." Alex squeezed her hands. "I agonized over it these past couple weeks to God. I am going to be moving and helping my parents get through all this. I am going to have a lot on my plate with all that and helping the girls adjust."

"I understand. I have a lot of things to adjust to as well. I feel overwhelmed with culture shock and being a new mom, but I really wish you wouldn't have to go," Rose said sadly.

"Oh Rose," Alex swept her into his arms and held her close. "As much as I want to, I can't ask you to be part of my future when I don't even know what that is. I'm sorry."

"Me too," Rose snuggled closer hoping to ease the ache in her heart. "This changes everything doesn't it?"

"I guess so, but I will still be your friend and we will see what God has for us in the future." He kissed her forehead.

"Definitely," Rose promised brushing away a tear.

"Kiss goodbye?" Alex asked softly.

In response to his request Rose stepped closer, and slid her arms around his neck. "I'd like that very much," she whispered.

"It was so hard saying goodbye to Alex," Rose confided to Michelle as the two of them watched the children playing under the sprinklers.

"I can only imagine," agreed Michelle. "But I think you both made a wise choice."

"I tried to tell myself that too, but what if we never get together?"

"You both will have to trust God on that. God has a perfect plan for your life," Michelle said.

"I know you're right. I like thinking about being with Alex but I know I'm nowhere near ready to think about marriage either."

"Marriage is such a huge step." Michelle agreed. "Has there ever been a situation like yours among your people before?" she asked.

"My sister was friends with a girl named Sarah, in Michigan, that got pregnant from a boy in her church, but he denied it and began dating another girl soon after. He married the other girl and Sarah bore the shame alone for a long time. There were so many bad rumors about her."

"Did she ever get married?"

"Yes, when her daughter was about seven. She married a guy from out of state, but that is the only case I know where the girl got married."

"Maybe you and Lane will get married someday." Michelle said.

"I don't think so. Lane made it clear that marrying me would mess up his life."

"Call me a hopeless romantic then," Michelle said. "But I love seeing families' together and happy endings."

Another Inspiritional Novel by
Barbara Yoder

The hardships of growing up in large Amish families had created a bond between Elizabeth and her best friend Rachel. In precious moments of free time they would escape to their favorite place by the creek to share their visions of the future. Rachel dreamed of romance while Elizabeth wondered what life would be like to not be Amish. But the girlhood dreams are shattered when Rachel is diagnosed with a serious illness. And the essence of their faith is tested as both girls come to grips with Rachel's illness. Elizabeth struggles to find the strength to cope with the tragic events as the mysteries of life and love unfold before her.

ISBN 1-58930-051-3 $12.95

To order additional copies of

To Be Loved
Or
Finding the Way

Please visit our website: www.amishechos.com

Books are also available through your local bookstore in the US

To contact the author:
Email: info@amishechos.com